Praise for Sandra Jones

"Sandra engages the reader with a range of emotions from hate to love and jealousy...This was definitely a fabulous read."

—Ramblings from This Chick on *Her Wicked Captain*

"Ms. Jones gets my top score of 5 fingers up & 10 toes & pretty please WRITE FASTER!"

—Avon Romance on *Her Wicked Captain*

"This book was an exciting read about gamblers and revenge. Dell and her wicked captain are exciting characters and I enjoyed the journey they embark upon together."

—Kilts and Swords on *Her Wicked Captain*

"Rory and Dell were great together. There was some really good sexual tension and the sex scenes were pretty steamy."

—The Blogger Girls on *Her Wicked Captain*

Look for these titles by Sandra Jones

Now Available:

The River Rogues
Her Wicked Captain

His Captive Princess

Sandra Jones

Samhain Publishing, Ltd.
11821 Mason Montgomery Road, 4B
Cincinnati, OH 45249
www.samhainpublishing.com

His Captive Princess

Print ISBN: 978-1-61922-840-5
Digital ISBN: 978-1-61922-445-2

Cover by Kim Killion

First Samhain Publishing, Ltd. electronic publication: April 2015
First Samhain Publishing, Ltd. print publication: April 2015

Dedication

For Scott and my father—my two favorite Welshmen.

Chapter One

Cantref Mawr, Deheubarth, Wales, Winter 1136 A.D.

Warren de Tracy had led battles on two different continents against formidable enemies of the Church and his Norman kings, and for his efforts he'd won spurs, a barony, more than a few scars and a complete lack of fear, which had served him well. Ironically, of all his venerable foes, a lowly dog killed him.

He watched the speckled greyhound resting on its dead master's chest, growling low at him, the stranger in its territory. The mongrel had already betrayed his Welsh owner's hiding spot in the dense thicket by protectively snarling at one of Warren's mounted knights. Then his hotheaded young soldier had wheeled back for the rebel enemy without caution, earning him a fatal arrow to the heart.

Making perhaps the worst tactical error of his life, Warren had followed to check on his fallen man. The dog, far from done, howled over its master's fate, thus calling attention to Warren's presence, too. That was when an arrow from God-only-knew-where in the surrounding woods took him by surprise, its force unseating him. Quick and efficient, these archers were so stealthy he'd never seen their faces.

Now left to travel afoot with a useless sword arm, Warren collapsed at the base of an ancient yew a few yards away from the two bodies. He stripped off his gloves and snapped the arrow's wooden shaft in half, leaving the barb lodged in his muscle. Ice-hot pain exploded through his chest.

"Sang Dieu!" He cradled his throbbing arm and waited, head swimming and shoulder bleeding, as the voices from the skirmish went silent.

All five of his men were dead. He felt it in his bones. Soon he would join them, but not nearly soon enough.

Ever since King Henry had died earlier that year, the Welsh princes had led revolts trying to take back lands they had lost in the Norman invasion. King Stephen, the new usurper, had ordered Warren to claim the Welsh Deheubarth camp of Dinefwr for Warren's own. All Warren had ever wanted was to gain the respect of his liege. King Stephen had also told Warren to take one of the Welsh princesses for a bride, which, along with promises of clemency and protection, would surely appease the locals. Furthermore, his liege had suggested, the widow of one of the recently fallen princes would be "receptive" to the offer.

How wrong the king had been.

If only Warren had known there would be a rebel spy waiting upon the shore when they landed. Now the entire conroi was dead as a result.

At least none of Warren's brothers had been with him this time. He could die without more shame hanging over his head. His half-brother would live to look after their little sister. With Warren dying honorably in battle, there would be no more questions of his loyalty, no more whispers of treason.

The dead soldier's quick end was a blessing compared to Warren's wound. The arrow in his shoulder wouldn't budge, proving it was a ruthless Norman barb, probably stolen from one of Warren's men, and the broken shaft offered no purchase with which to maneuver it. Each time he touched the splintered wood, a burst of fire spread through his chest. His heavy sword was meant for hacking bone, not useful for quickening his death, but perhaps he could knock himself unconscious while he waited for the arms of everlasting rest.

He leaned against the tree and battered the back of his skull, but the beating only made his head ache and his vision blur. The agony of his shoulder remained.

He closed his eyes before the reeling made him vomit.

Despite the absence of wind, the nearby trees rustled softly. Warren cracked an eye open. A hooded rebel stood near De Gouin's body. As silently as the first, another dark-hooded figure dropped from the branches above. Dressed in deerskin chausses and heavy tunics, they studied the soldier's corpse. *Bon sang!* Welsh rebels. Or Cymreig, as they called themselves. The smaller one nudged the dead knight's arm with a booted foot. Bows resting casually on their backs, the pair hadn't seemed to notice Warren.

His left hand tightened around the sword's hilt. One good throw would fell one of the lightweight bastards, but he had no way of fending off the other.

As if sensing Warren's intentions, the greyhound's growl deepened, and it glanced uncertainly between Warren and the rebels. The archers were still too far away to hear, too absorbed in retrieving his soldier's weapons, but the dog might change that. His barking would bring them around, turning their attention to Warren. He couldn't let that happen. He was ready to die but not to be shamefully taken alive as a hostage for the local chieftain, where he would surely find unimaginable tortures.

He adjusted his grip on the sword in his left hand. His arm shook from the loss of blood.

The beast hunkered over his master's body, putting more of its belly on top of the man's chest. Caesar, Warren's own trained mastiff, would do the same. Now staring into this animal's brown eyes, he saw unwavering loyalty and trust, so like Caesar's.

The greyhound licked the dead Welshman's face, and the sight put a knot in Warren's throat. He'd never harmed an animal before, nor would he this day.

Before the wary tension in his muscles could relax, the dog woofed in his direction.

Damned traitor!

The enemies swiveled around. Assessing the situation, they drew their swords.

In Warren's foggy vision, the two swarmed toward him like sylvan elves, multiplying as yet more rebels fell from the tree, at least a half-dozen of his enemies.

The first pair stood over him with weapons extended, while the newcomers surrounded their own fallen warrior and his canine.

"Gorthwr fud." The one who'd kicked De Gouin spoke at him in a puzzle of confusing sounds, but the sneered tone was perfectly clear. More puzzling than the guttural language Warren had been trying to decipher since arriving on the Glamorgan shore a few days ago was the fact that the rebel's voice was female, low and husky. The accented tones would be interesting, he reckoned, if they weren't so full of hate.

He blinked hard to clear the cobwebs in his vision. A pale oval shape loomed before him, and soon he focused on a pair of dark golden eyes in a face with skin that seemed to glow as if lit by moonlight. She dropped her hood for a better look at him, revealing wild plaits of flaming red hair, which dangled around her perfect face.

"Aye. I called you a dumb Norman and now you've proven it," she drawled.

He tried to lift his sword but the weight was more than he could wield. The red sprite above him gestured with a small pointing finger. He followed it and found her deerskin boot firmly planted on his blade.

"I'll finish him for you, *Dywysoges.* He killed Iolo ap Rhys." The second hooded archer was also a woman, with black hair worn in a single braid. She grabbed his wounded shoulder with a rough hand, pushing the broken arrow deeper with her thumb as she held her sword against his heart.

A wave of pain and nausea wrenched Warren. He thrust his chest against the blade, grimacing as the metal pierced his skin, determined not to empty his stomach in front of the dark-headed one and her fiery companion as he welcomed the swift death.

"Nay. This one *wants* to die, Nest." The red maid pushed the other woman's sword aside. Then, crouching in front of Warren, she studied him through narrowed eyes and stroked her full lips with the tip of her finger, thinking. The scent of the forest and wildflowers drifted from her skin. Whether brave or stupid, she left the weapon in his hand carelessly unattended as she watched him.

Ah, but she was right in her courage. He posed little threat to anyone now.

Staring at her mouth, Warren felt something within him stir. It had been a long time since he'd touched a woman's lips, but by the rood, to lust at such a time!

The men hailed to the women in their tongue and the dark maid rallied them.

Red rested her sword across her thighs. "It would be wrong to kill him this way. We'll take him to the castell and let Lew decide what to do with him." She shrugged, drawing his eye to her chest and further proof she was indeed female. Her curves tightened the leather tunic in the movement. "Besides, he spared the life of Iolo's dog."

"That's because he *is* a dog." A beastly black-headed man pushed through the newcomers and kicked Warren in the ribs. "Norman bastard!"

The blow knocked him to the ground, rattling his teeth. Warren tasted blood and his tongue smarted from where he'd bitten it. His ribcage ached from the impact, but it would take much worse to kill him quickly.

Red spoke rapidly in her language at the barrel-chested soldier and the chastised man reddened, ducking his chin. He and another warrior grabbed Warren's arms, disarming him, and hoisted him to his feet. His head reeled with the pain of the hasty movement.

Following the lady archers, the other men carried the body of the one they called Iolo as the dog trailed behind. Warren concentrated on his feet, walking obediently between his captors. If these Welsh rebels respected Red as much as it appeared, mayhap he knew how to draw their wrath to hasten his death.

The group marched him into the woods. Watching the exposed roots of the forest glen below his boots, he stumbled once, twice, then a third time, making sure they assumed him too weak to be a threat. His captors were large men, perhaps the best warriors of their tribe, and Warren prayed they had hostile tempers to match.

Lulled into complacency, one of the brigands' hands loosened on his arm, and Warren had his chance. Breaking free, he grabbed a handful of Red's braids and tangled his fingers in the silky plaited coils. She cried out, flailing her arms, but he dragged her against him as he fell backward, pulling her down on top of him.

The warriors' retaliation was prompt—a slightly less ignoble death than betrayal by dog. First, Red jabbed an elbow into his groin, but he held tight. The men responded, kicking his head and sides.

Strike, kick, strike...

He shut his eyes and slid toward unconsciousness on the tide of agony, his senses closing with the pleasant wildflower fragrance of Red's hair in his face and her soft, wriggling body atop his.

Princess Eleri ferch Gruffydd stretched out her legs and sat back, listening to the River Tywi from her perch on a rock in the moonlight. Beside her, Lew fell silent—so mature for a youth of seven and ten—although he was often quiet when he meditated on his burdens as the Prince of Deheubarth.

Or when he lost himself in memories of his older brother, Owain, her late husband, gone these past six months.

Eleri concentrated on the riverbanks, pushing Lew to the periphery of her mind, and searched for motion in the darkness, looking for a sign or portent of warning for her husband's people. But thank Goddess, this night there seemed to be no warnings, only the unnerving sound of restless birds in the surrounding trees, stirring on their midnight roosts.

She rubbed the back of her head where her scalp still ached and tingled from the *Gorthwr*'s grip on her hair.

Apparently taking her movement as permission to speak, the prince broke his silence. "Is the *cyhyraeth* here again? Do you see her?"

Eleri shook her head. "No. We'll have no more deaths tomorrow. I trow I should have let our captive die. Iolo's wife is keen to kill him herself."

The new widow had spat on Eleri when she learned her part in sparing the Norman's life. Being as Eleri was still considered a member of the royal Deheubarth family, even one whose husband was no longer living, the action was a punishable offense and brought the grieving woman a swift sentence of a sennight in chains.

If only I'd let Sayer finish him…

But no, once again she'd given her brother-in-law an opportunity to exert his authority. A chance he was rarely allowed in the meetings of his own Council. Besides, she hated the idea of allowing any Norman to have something he wanted—even if it was death.

Lew fidgeted beside her again, rubbing his arms where his battle mail had likely chafed him. She smelled the minty scent of the healer's poultice on his skin. "Do you not think my first attack was a success, Eleri?" He looked at her expectantly, then away when she would not answer. Neither reveled in the uprising the Council had demanded. "Iolo was the only fallen warrior we had. I believe it is because we took the Normans by complete surprise. No one else was even wounded. But… are you for certes this man killed Iolo?"

"Nay, but there was another Norman's body nearby. It had the looks of vengeance to me."

Lew extended his arm and opened his hand to her. A flat piece of metal lay on his palm. "This is a Norman barb taken from the prisoner's wound. Mayhap he killed his own man."

"Mayhap. One of his men must've wanted him dead…unless the bastard fell on his own arrow." She tried to smile but felt no real humor while looking at the grim arrowhead, still crusted with the man's blood.

Lew chuckled and turned the metal in his hand. "Well, I suppose I should call the council and ask what they advise, but I wager they'll choose death for the Norman in return for my brother's life, as well as Iolo's."

Eleri nodded, feeling another wave of grief. She hugged her knees and watched the ripple of the moon's reflection on the river.

Lew stood and left for the great hall.

She should have said something to console him, something to cool his hunger for retribution. They could not kill the entire Norman army. The loss of Lew's beloved brother in battle had hurt him deeply—even more than it had her, the wife Owain had bedded once and abandoned.

But Eleri wanted revenge too. Thanks to the Normans, Owain was dead, and having no children, she now depended on Lew's friendship, her servants' unflinching allegiance, and the generosity of the Deheubarth people.

The foreigner had not hurt Eleri when he'd grabbed her. His hard, muscular body had broken her fall, and her sore scalp would heal on the morrow. Still, she had no pity for him or his kind. When he'd looked up at her through defiant eyes of ocean blue, she'd felt intrigued by the resolve she'd seen in their depths—mayhap even appreciative of his strong, masculine features, much like Owain's—but feelings of guilt quickly overtook her. Besides, he would've hurt her later if he had a chance. Knowing that, she'd wanted to do as Nest had done and twist the arrow deeper in the bastard's chest until he screamed.

Yet he would not scream.

Eleri had sat outside the room while the healer had cut the metal free from the prisoner's body. The witnesses to his procedure had said he'd chewed his tongue, fought the bonds that restrained him, and cursed them in his foul Norman language. But he'd never once broken down to pleas or crying.

Perhaps he was made of stone, through and through. A heartless invader. Most of his kind were, stealing land for their king and displacing the Cymreig principalities. They took, killed and raped their way through Cymru until they had everything they wanted. And they always would.

Once the prisoner was dead, her people would feel some relief at having one less foreigner on their lands, and would no doubt take comfort knowing that the enemy's king would have no one left alive to ask who attacked his men.

Suddenly nauseous, Eleri clutched her stomach. She needed to distance herself from the council and the prisoner. Fighting was easy. Torture, she abhorred.

She stood and wiped at the grit clinging to her drawers. She would feel better once she'd changed into her nightclothes and climbed into her bed.

Splash!

She spun toward the sound of water. Her heart in her throat, she focused in the darkness at the form taking shape across the river. Blue skin, sagging and shriveled, glistened on a skeletal female body wading into the current up to its ghostly knees.

Eleri felt cold sweat break on her skin and swallowed. *Gwrach y Rhibyn.* The ugly woman.

She longed to shout at the horrid wretch, to beg her to leave them alone. But it was no use. Although Eleri had witnessed the sight countless times, the hag of the mist never paid her any attention.

As Eleri now stood hugging herself from revulsion and the sheer terror of anticipation, the *cyhyraeth* began her ritual.

First, she stared through orb-less eyes into the distance. Then her lips turned down at the corners, trembling, and she wept as she washed her birdlike hands.

Eleri listened for the fateful omen, tears pricking her eyes, too, and then there it was—

"Fy mab, fy mab!" Gwrach y Rhibyn sobbed as she wrung her bony fingers. *"Fy mab, fy mab!" My son, my son.* A chill went up Eleri's spine as she brushed the moisture from her eyes with the back of her hand. *Nay. She must be wrong.* Then as silent as death, the creature rose from the water in a beam of frosty blue light and vanished back into the black forest.

Eleri let out her breath. Just once she would like to see the ugly woman appear and disappear without saying a word. But it was never to be. There was always a Cymreig victim.

Yestereve, Gwrach had cried, "My husband, my husband," leaving Eleri to only guess which of the married warriors would fall in their planned ambush, and no way to warn Iolo before he died. This time, Gwrach's prediction left Eleri no doubt whose death had been foretold. There were no sons among her husband's warriors. Only Lew. The youngest.

Nay! Not Lew.

The prince was alive and well, no sign of illness to kill him. Could he have somehow sealed this fate by allowing the death of the prisoner? The Norman was the last of his conroi. His fatal end at Lew's hands would be noted by his king. Other soldiers would come to avenge the slaughter. The Council would then blame the mistake on her brother-in-law even though it wasn't his idea. Ultimately, the prisoner's death could bring Lew's.

Of course. That was it. Even if it wasn't the reason, she couldn't take any chances.

Eleri broke into a run for the great hall, praying she wouldn't be too late.

Their captive *must* live.

Chapter Two

By Deheubarth law, as their *dywysoges*, or princess, Eleri could fight alongside her men, but she had no say in the meetings of the Council. She found the exclusion absurd, and had needed to remind herself that she wasn't their kind.

Born to the royal Aberffraw family of Gwynedd, she had been allowed to address her father's court at home, with its mix of noble and baseborn men such as the leaders, lords and fighters of the Deheubarth. It rankled knowing that in her husband's castell she was considered less than these men.

With these venomous thoughts thrumming behind her temples, she charged through the heavy wooden doors of the great hall and pushed her way between the shoulders of the warriors to reach the table of the mighty lords.

She stopped directly across from Lew's chair and bowed with a formal air they never used in private. "Your Highness, forgive me."

Perhaps it was her father's fault for raising her to think for herself. Or perhaps it was Owain's. Sometimes she allowed her late husband's resentment of some of his kin to sway to her opinion, clouding her judgment, but she couldn't help thinking that had it not been for the arrogance and weakness of the Deheubarth, the kingdoms of Cymru would still be under the rule of their native people.

Standing beside her, Lord Vaughn bristled. "*Dywysoges*, you should not be here."

He put a gloved hand on her arm and she wrenched away. His touch revolted her, along with his deep-set eyes that lingered on her longer than the offensive hand.

"And you should not be addressing me." While Owain was still warm in his grave, Vaughn, his cousin, had tried to coax his way into her bed. She snapped her gaze away from him, focusing on the more important matter at hand, and addressed Lew again. "Your Highness, I ask you to spare the prisoner's life. He must not be killed."

Shocked silence followed as those in attendance stared at her in disbelief.

"My Prince," Owain's most trusted advisor, Gareth ap Huw, interrupted from his chair, his silver hair creating a halo within the folds of his cloak's hood, "this is a council matter. The princess cannot be allowed to speak."

Lew stared at Eleri, and she implored him silently. In front of his ruling council, the prince's stony countenance gave no indication of his concern, but he leaned forward almost imperceptibly. "Have you news of our captive to share?"

"Aye." She glanced around the table at their audience. There was naught for it; she must talk openly of her vision. Yet there were those in the Council who thought Lew weak. An untried ruler, every move he made was measured and compared to men with more experience. Telling these untrustworthy snakes that the wraith had predicted Lew's death might be a mistake. She chose a different explanation. "I saw the Ugly Woman, and she cried for…the Norman. She would not do that if his blood wasn't Cymreig." One by one, she met the eyes of each man around the circle as the lie soured on her tongue.

The room exploded in grumbles of denial. "The Norman has Cymreig blood?" "Impossible!"

"How is it impossible?" She exhaled angrily, hoping to hide her anxiousness for Lew with her notorious temper. And anyway, it wasn't a farfetched lie. Seventy years ago, William of Normandy had spread his barons throughout the land, encouraging his kind to marry royal Cymreig daughters.

Gareth traced his chin thoughtfully. "It's no more impossible than a princess of Gwynedd marrying a prince of Deheubarth."

"Or a Norman raping a Cymreig woman, and stealing the by-blow to raise as one of theirs," Vaughn declared. "And if that be the case, the bastard isn't worthy of our mercy."

"You must never ignore the wraith's omens. Remember the others…" Gareth glanced meaningfully at the wooden walls of the hall, where the images of past battles had been preserved in fine tapestries. Kings, princes, noblemen, children and paupers—all those from the Tywi valley who'd fought and died. According to legend, the Ugly Woman had foretold many of the losses, and each generation had at least one visionary whom she visited.

Eleri wouldn't wish her so-called visitor upon her greatest foe. What person wanted to be told when a neighbor, friend or family member would die?

"What were her exact words?" Lew asked, his hands tightening around the oak armrests of his chair.

Eleri wiped her clammy hands on her tunic and glanced around at her audience again. Prickles ran down her back, but she had no other course of action but to lie. "'My husband…'"

Vaughn huffed, crossing his arms over his chest. "And this is what tells you it's the Norman? It could be any of a number of married warriors—"

"No." Eleri shook her head emphatically. "No one is sick. No one is heading into battle. Unless one of our men is about to be murdered, the only soul in danger is the Norman's."

Some of the men murmured to each other. She strained to hear, but couldn't make out their words.

Lew's gaze never wavered from her and the gravity of the situation shone in his pale gray eyes. He nodded slowly. "As you say, Princess Eleri. The vision is yours to interpret. The Norman will live and remain as our prisoner."

"My wife says he has a strong body. He'll make a good slave," Simon, the bard, agreed. His wife had been the healer who'd removed the arrow from the man.

"Keeping him alive would bring *us* closer to death. He could escape and take word back to his people. We killed unarmed men. What do you think his king will do when he hears of this?" Vaughn snarled.

Privately she'd advised Lew not to ambush the Normans, but his Council had been adamant. Then upon finding the invaders' numbers much smaller than they'd been told—a party of four men against the men of the entire Cantref Mawr—she'd urged them to desist.

But this time Vaughn had a point. Eleri shuffled her feet irritably. "Mayhap his mission was one of treaty, and if that's true, he could easily be a nobleman. Do we want to kill a man we might use to trade for those of our men captured at Cardigan?" She was grasping for excuses, but these thick-headed men would know no different.

Ewen, one of Vaughn's men, slapped a meaty hand on the table. "I say we kill him now. Are we being led by a female, as well as a boy?"

Lew shoved his chair back from the table. "Would you have spoken to Owain thusly?" Thrusting back his shoulders, the young prince regarded Eleri again. "He will live."

Eleri released her breath and fought the impulse to smile.

Gareth cleared his throat. "But if he's not a nobleman, his king may storm our walls, caring not in the least if the prisoner dies."

Vaughn hovered behind her. She could feel his hot, sour breath on her neck. "Your people make use of slaves, Princess. My men will take him to Gwynedd. If he makes the journey alive, the Normans will have to deal with them for his return. It would not be our problem in Deheubarth."

A murmur of approval rumbled around the table along the bobbing heads of the elders.

A journey such as that was difficult for even the healthiest men. A wounded man in the hands of Vaughn's vicious curs, who detested all Norman scourge? He would be dead in no time at all, and his passing would bring Lew's as the old wraith had foretold.

Poor Lew could still be overthrown as an ineffective ruler if the matter wasn't handled carefully.

"It is settled." The prince squeezed his pale hand in a fist. "We will give him three days to heal, then send him with Lord Vaughn's men."

Eleri lowered her eyes. Vaughn wanted the *Gorthwr*'s blood on his hands, wanted Lew's blood on his hands. But most of all, Vaughn wanted her.

With Owain gone and Lew deposed, he would have everything he desired.

Warren's resolve crumbled. The persistent tickle on his nose demanded to be scratched, and no matter how much pain the movement cost him, he would quell it.

Twisting in his rope bonds with his hands tied high above his head, he rubbed his nose against his forearm. The rope scalded his wrists where his skin had rubbed raw. Alas, his bare arms gave him no relief.

Mayhap he would go mad in captivity with these barbarians. Mayhap he had already.

The tight timbers of the cell's windowless walls prevented him from seeing whether it was night or day. Only the drop in temperature and the lack of visitors told him it was night. The tribe's healer hinted that he would be leaving soon, though not in any words he understood. None of his visitors had spoken in his language since the day he'd been captured. He'd pieced together the fact he was being moved when the old woman had fed him that night, washed and returned his clothing, and had even placed a decorative brace of an iron bull in his fire—the pagan symbol he recognized for virility.

Why would they want me healthy?

The question had kept him awake for what seemed like ages as he stared into the slowly dying embers.

Being released was the worst that could befall him. To be found alive by his king equated to treason by his liege's thinking. Even though Warren had outwardly shunned his half-sister, Empress Matilda, in her quest to take the crown from King Stephen, his loyalty was still in doubt. Gladly he would cast in his die with Matilda, the true heir named by King Henry himself, if doing so wouldn't put his family in jeopardy. Warren had done all he could to protect them. His dying would finally make them blameless and wealthy to boot. The perfect answer to all their woes.

"Be still, *Gorthwr*," a cool female voice uttered from the shadows.

He twisted toward the source. "*Par le sang Dieu*, how did you—"

"Shhhh."

He felt weight press the bed beside him. Turning his head, his cheek rested against soft leather stretched tight across what might've been a woman's thigh if he guessed correctly.

The idea warmed him immensely. He chuckled. "Ah, so you've kept me alive to come have your way with me, *Mademoiselle Roux*?" At least he hoped it was she and not her unpleasant companion, the one called Nest.

"You must not speak to the *Dywysoges*!" a man growled.

A sharp dagger's tip pinched against Warren's throat, punctuating the order. Warren could make out the outlines of the pair hovering over him. He wished he could see the sultry sprite's expression and read her thoughts on the subject. If he wasn't mistaken the male was the one who'd beaten him within an inch of his life.

What was the meaning of this word "*dywysoges*" they kept calling her?

"Well if I may, perhaps I could address *you* then?" Warren softened his tone to the measure he used with his varlet back at home in England. "Pierce the jugular, if you would. It's quicker that way. I could direct you if you're not familiar."

"I assure you, Norman, I know many ways to kill a man." Nevertheless, the rebel took the knife away. He whispered to the woman, "Your Highness, the prisoner would be easier to transport if he was dead. Would you like me to—"

"No, Sayer. You know you cannot," she murmured.

"'Your Highness'?" Warren jerked in astonishment, pulling against his bonds. The ropes chafed his raw skin, sending a fresh wave of pain down his arms. "You're of royal blood?"

She leaned over him, reaching for his bonds. "Hush! In addition to your arrow wound, I trow your tongue has healed as well these past days. It would behoove you to use it less and just be grateful you're alive."

Her breasts hovered inches above his face. In fact, if he lifted his head, he could bury his face between them. What would she do, this spirited wench, if he chose to do so? He would've enjoyed finding out if circumstances had been different. "I'd rather be dead than be a prisoner. But first…I'll kiss your feet if you'd scratch my nose."

She made a choking noise in her throat that almost sounded like amusement.

He felt a tug at his ropes and the friction of a knife. By the saints, she was freeing him. He couldn't allow it.

Air stung his raw skin as soon as one of his wrists came loose. With his one arm still useless in its restraints, he shot out his free hand and clutched her forearm. Using all his strength, he turned her over beneath him, wedging her between his torso and the bed. Nose to nose, he could make out her eyes gone wide with shock in the darkness. "No!" he growled. "Do not let me leave here alive."

Suddenly, her warrior was upon him and his knife back against Warren's throat. "Get off the princess, you cur!"

The woman's blade touched his chest plate. She could dispatch him with ease. Her arms were strong and lean. Her body was far from frail, and he recalled her skillful defeat of his conroi. She twisted beneath his pelvis defensively, and the grinding of her soft mound awoke his sex. Shame heated his cheeks at his sudden need and dark desires. This one time, he would allow himself to speak his mind. "If you release me, Princess, I'll go to Kidwelly and inform my commanders what has befallen my five men at the hands of you and your people. The king will strike at the subjects of Cantref Mawr with vengeance such as you've never known."

Her expression shifted from stark panic to slow derision as her saucy lips curved up at one corner. "You think I don't know what you're capable of?" Her eyes flashed downward meaningfully, and he knew she'd noted the turn of his wicked thoughts. "You want to have your way with me. To tear my clothing from my body and part my legs. But you know nothing of my people, Norman. You haven't even bothered to learn the language—" she broke off, slurring in Welsh at her vassal.

The burly guard grabbed Warren's bandaged shoulder, twisting it back until bile climbed in his throat. "*Umpff*!" While he convulsed in pain, the woman slipped loose and turned him on his back, pinning his groin beneath two very sharp knees. He hissed through his teeth, "*Par les saints*!"

If he'd been successful in his mission, this devil-wench would've been his *bride*?

"You are my prisoner, knight." She planted the flat of her hand against his neck, leaving no doubt of her desire for domination as her angry pulse drummed against his skin. "I am the Princess of Deheubarth, widow of Prince Owain ap Daffyd, murdered by your Norman peers. It will be my pleasure keeping you alive. We're taking you to those who will do with you what they will. I care not. Until then, you are my dog. My captive. My slave. And you *will* obey!"

Chapter Three

Eleri stared over the campfire at the Norman's profile as she ground fresh mint into the rest of the paste with a wooden spoon. After a grueling night and day of travel on foot while leading the horses through the thorny scrub, they sat resting as Nest watched the path they'd taken in case Vaughn or his men had followed. Sayer gathered kindling in the forest for the cold night's fire, leaving Eleri alone guarding the captive. Meanwhile the gravity of her actions sank in.

They'd stolen the prisoner to deliver him alive to her father, and there would likely be outrage at her decision.

Oddly, the Norman formed a proud figure from the side, sitting in the weeds with his broad shoulders back, head high and hands relaxed even in the tight bonds Nest had gleefully cinched around his raw wrists behind him. Despite the leather hood they'd used to blind him, he had the perfect posture and bearing of a nobleman at court.

The possibility of his royal birthright had grown more likely in Eleri's mind ever since they'd slipped from the castell at nightfall, unnoticed. He hadn't complained much about his circumstances, hadn't even tried to barter for his freedom. If he was a member of the Norman king's family, he should at least ask for a ransom price.

Unless he wasn't the idiot Eleri had first thought. Perhaps he realized they weren't interested in his money.

The prisoner's calm demeanor might be more of his trickery. She wouldn't put it past him. He was no doubt waiting for them to make a mistake, then he would attempt escape. His promise for retaliation lingered in her thoughts…along with the things she'd claimed he wanted to do to her.

Though it had been hours ago, she still felt the heat of his breath on her neck, his long legs of iron tangled with hers and the alarming hardening of his body—something not even Owain had shown her in their short time together when he'd come to their marriage bed. The stranger's touch had brought back longings and desire she'd hoped to keep forgotten.

Made her wish for things she would never have.

Arrogant cur! She shouldn't have risked coming so near him. And yet she must approach him again. His presence and cryptic words created too many questions.

Gathering her courage, Eleri left the fire, taking her bowl of herbs and an extra fur. Catching Sayer's glower as he stomped back into the clearing with an armload of twigs, she patted the dagger strapped on her hip and arched an eyebrow, daring him to argue with her. He shook his head as he dropped the wood and trudged back out into the darkness. He wouldn't be far away as she interrogated the Norman, probably listening for any hint of the prisoner's disobedience.

Stealthily creeping up behind the man, she heard a soft recitation coming from beneath his hood. *"Oh, to be a sparrow-hawk, a goshawk. I'd fly to my love."* An Occitan poem from his court, she realized, and her heart felt a tiny dart. She'd learned the foreign language of troubadours in her own father's keep. So strange to think the dreaded enemy cared for such trivialities. But then, she knew nothing about him. He could've left a family behind, a wife and children. She focused on the foreign words, translating as she folded her legs to sit opposite him. *"Touch her, embrace her, kiss her lips so soft, sweeten and soothe my pain. I like it near the fountain. I trained a falcon. Spread her wings so wide—"*

The words took a naughty turn. Face heating, Eleri cleared her throat before she might endure worse.

His head slanted, but he gave no start. His voice lifted. "Do not fear you've lost your ability to take me by surprise, my lady. 'Tis strong medicine you have there, to penetrate this foul covering."

Eleri hugged the bowl tighter. He'd sensed her coming and recited his bawdy love poem a'purpose!

She braced for a fight, preparing to cast aside her bowl if need be and draw her dagger. But to extract the information she wanted, she would have to wheedle it from him carefully. She forced friendliness into her voice. "If you behave yourself, I'll let you have some relief."

"Ah, I somehow knew 'twas Red, not Nest, come to visit." His chest expanded on a sigh of satisfaction.

Another wave of heat fanned through her. Anger, she hoped.

"Aye, I'll behave, as you say, my lady, but I doubt you're here to offer the relief I'm thinking of."

Blood boiling, she yanked off his hood, and his dark hair fell loose, framing his rugged face. He cringed against the firelight, meager though it was. Perhaps unjustly, they'd kept him under the hood for the entire day. Now Eleri could scrutinize his looks in the light for the first time since they'd taken him.

His face was built in ridges and angles, with a small bump in the bridge of his nose, and thick dark brows marred by a narrow scar through their luxuriousness. Yet the imperfections in no way detracted from his handsome appearance. When his eyes opened fully and fastened on her, she felt the air siphon from her lungs. Cool ocean blue, as she recalled, but now she noticed a trace of brown near the irises as if his maker hadn't fully decided which color to paint them. It lent him an air of mystery and made him fascinating to stare at, if only he wasn't such a brute.

She frowned, remembering why she was angry.

His perfectly bowed lips curved at her expression. "I meant the *relief* you might provide by finishing me…er, with that dagger of yours. But if you've a mind to do otherwise, my stamina isn't fully returned. Still, I would like to get my hand in your hair again. Mayhap if you aided me—"

"Enough!" She glanced over her shoulder, burning with mortification. The others were nowhere in sight—a thought that both comforted and discomposed her. Then returning to him, she hissed, "See here, if you continue to speak to me so, I'll have Sayer attend you, and I vow he'll leave the hood on."

His jaw tightened. "Well, then I shall hold my tongue, as you wish. I've had more than enough of your guard's help for one day." Some of the color leaked from his tawny face, and Eleri wondered if he was remembering the times Sayer had aided him when he'd had to urinate. Fearing the prisoner would try to escape, they'd kept his hands tied then, too.

"I've brought you some cover." She lifted a corner of the soft fur blanket held in her lap. "The night will be colder than you are used to in Normandy, I warrant. And here's a poultice for your wound."

"I'm from Devon," he corrected, then sniffed. "Mint?"

"Aye. Also honey, oak, verbena and juniper berries."

"Are you trying to make me tasty for the birds?" His voice was dry, though not entirely bitter.

She bit the inside of her lip. *He would not make her smile!* She smoothed back a lock of hair from her brow that had escaped her plaits. Then she averted her gaze to the pungent green glob in the bowl. "Actually, it's more to cover your smell."

"Your healer bathed me only yestereve. I trow I smell better than the three of you." He arched an eyebrow, clearly affronted, and again Eleri was struck by his highborn mannerism.

She gave the goo a stir with the wooden spoon. "I do not doubt your cleanliness, but we will soon be passing through other cantrefs that do not belong to the Deheubarth. Would you have them recognizing a Norman?" His eyes narrowed, thinking, and she hastened to add, "Aye, perhaps you would. But we would rather not lose you to them. And you must remember, we've not mistreated you, but other Cymreig would. Your time with them would not end quickly enough. Torture, maiming, your eyes, tongue—"

"*Oui. Oui.* I take your meaning. But where you're taking me, is it any better? How do I know you're not bringing me to someone who'll take pleasure in my pain?"

She couldn't stop her smile. "You don't know. Consider this your penance for being a *Gorthwr fud* and for all the crimes your kind has visited upon Cymru."

"Wales," he translated aloud. "And I didn't come to Wales to do you or the Deheubarth any wrong."

"Why did you come here then?" Her heart started as excitement ran through her. Perhaps she'd have her answers simply for the asking.

"Untie me and I'll tell you."

Or not.

Eleri rested the spoon in the bowl and dipped her middle finger into the slime. "And have you attack me again? I think not." His gaze followed her movement as she lifted the poultice to her nose, sniffed, then touched it to the tip of her tongue. "You're right. 'Tis almost tasty."

He sighed. "You know, I *am* hungry. Mayhap I would answer your questions for food."

Eleri snorted. He would rather die by blade than from starvation? The healer had told her he'd eaten enough for three men after he'd recovered his strength. "I'll bring you something to eat once you've answered my questions. What were you doing here?"

"How about a trade? An answer for an answer."

"A princess does not bargain with a slave."

His expression darkened. A tiny line formed between his serious eyes. He wanted to tell her who he was. She could sense the tension of his powerful body, the indignity he suffered for his present situation and… his hate for her.

"Fine. I will die of hunger if you do not answer my questions. They say the end from starvation comes in pleasant slumber." He lifted his good shoulder. "If you wish to keep me alive, my first question is your name, my princess."

"All right, Norman. You've made your point. I'll answer your questions because I have naught to hide from the likes of you." She tossed the fur across his lap and put the bowl down as he raised his head, confidence glowing in his damnable, imperfectly handsome face. Putting her hands on him again both repelled and intrigued her, a mistake she didn't want to repeat. She pushed the bowl beside him and freed her dagger from her belt. "I'll cut you loose so you can apply your poultice, but one sign of your trickery and I'll make you a gelding."

He nodded. "You have my word. Another question, where are we now? 'Tis cooler, though we're still in a valley."

Perceptive. She cut the first loop of his ropes, hoping to have enough left to bind him later. "We're on the northern border of Cantref Mawr, about to cross into Buellt, the Norman stronghold, but we're still several days from where you're headed."

Flexing his big hands in front of him, he scowled. Half to himself, he murmured, "William de Braose, the Marcher Lord. Loyal to Stephen. He has holdings in Devon too."

"Aye, but do not get any grand ideas about escape. I'll put an arrow in your back to match the wound in the front. Besides, we're in the woods of the Britons. The true people of Buellt bow to no ruler, least of all a Norman." She gave him her nastiest grin to dash any hopes he had of running. "Now my turn. Who are you?"

He favored his shoulder as he stretched his sinewy arms. "Warren de Tracy. And you are?"

She shook her head. "I care not for your name. Who *are* you?"

His eyes widened, and then one eyebrow arched with appreciation. "You wish to beg a ransom for my life?"

"No more questions from you. 'Tis my turn."

"I am of no consequence…to anyone now. Go ahead, ask for a ransom. The king will laugh." His teeth, perfect and white, gleamed in a grin, yet concern riddled his brow. His healthy smile said more for his birthright than words ever could.

He hooked his thumbs in the hem of his long tunic and drew it up revealing a bronze, muscle-clad torso. Then he slowly pulled one arm free and the next.

This handsome soldier with his insolence and cryptic answers was treading on her patience—which she did not possess. She shouldn't be sitting with her enemy, shouldn't be admiring his sculpted chest, his fine smile, his poetry, or his intriguing blue-brown eyes.

Pulse ticking in her throat, she snatched the bowl and backed away. "Never mind. Don't answer. I'll bind your hands again and you can die from your wound. Of that you will suffer in painful misery, for certes."

He casually rolled onto a knee and sighed. "Very well. My family had connections to the late king, Henry Beauclerc, who as you know died just last month. Stephen of Blois, his...*successor*...sent me here in the hopes of claiming Castle Dinefwr."

"And we were to simply give it to your men for asking?"

He chewed on his lip, his speculative gaze traipsing down her length.

Her heart skittered nervously.

"I never said he was a wise king." His mouth quirked. "Now answer my first question." He took the bowl and, holding it one hand, peered at the wound beneath his bandages. He scowled at what he saw, then took a scoop of the aromatic herbs and rubbed it under his bandage. "*Votre nom*, Princess of Deheubarth. Your name?" He watched her beneath his lashes as his hand made slow, wide circles on his smooth skin.

Don't tell him. He doesn't need to know. Don't—

"Eleri!" Nest hissed from the woods, emerging on the back of one of Lew's coursers at a brisk pace. Her eyes grew round when she noted the unbound prisoner. Reining her mount before them, she corrected herself, "Princess, 'tis Vaughn and his men!"

Nest circled Warren on her courser—his horse, Bane, taken alive in the skirmish, *thank God*—which was snuffling and tossing its black mane in its excitement to be near him.

"What is he doing untied?" She drew her blade on him. "He'll slow us down and alert Lord Vaughn."

Ah! Warren observed the princess's reaction and found her alabaster skin becoming even whiter. He should've asked the most important question plaguing him that day: why were they leaving the castell in the middle of the night in such haste? But he'd let his lust take the lead, first inquiring after her name—as if such mattered anymore.

Yet now he had the answer to both.

Eleri.

"Who is Lord Vaughn and why should I wish to alert him?" He bent to retrieve his tunic.

"Shut up!" Nest halted his progress, keeping her mount between him and the princess. "We ought to let him have you."

"What is happening here?" Burly Sayer jogged into the firelight.

"They've caught up with us," Nest growled.

"I knew we made too many stops!" Sayer spat at Warren's feet, and the white spittle trickled off the toe of his boot. "I should've draped the Norman's worthless hide over my horse's saddle and let him piss on himself—"

"Sayer! This isn't helping." The princess gazed up at Nest, seizing her reins. "Take all four horses, lead Vaughn's men toward the Valley of Flowers. They'll think we're headed for the safety of the monastery. Then leave the road when you can and circle back."

The dark maid drew her black cloak around her shoulders, fixing Warren with a wary look, then made a short bow as if she'd argued with the princess before and thought better of making the same mistake. "Aye, *Dywysoges*," she grumbled.

While Nest thundered away with the horses, Eleri and Sayer kicked dirt into the fire until the flames went out.

Warren pulled his tunic on and retrieved the fur, as well as the rope and hood, which he tucked in the waist of his breeches while his captors had their backs to him.

"That's all we can do." The princess put a staying hand on Sayer's arm, then slung her bow and quiver over her shoulder. "The bowl."

Warren moved aside as Sayer barreled by and buried the remaining evidence of their camp beneath dead leaves.

"Can you climb?" Eleri asked.

Warren glanced down at the woman, who'd appeared at his side as if by more of her elf-like magic. "Climb?" He surveyed his surroundings, his first real chance to do so since she'd removed his hood. Without the fire, he could barely make out the yew trees around them and their ancient, winding limbs reaching to the inky sky.

"Sayer." She spun away with a deep sigh, taking his silence for an answer. "We'll take this one. 'Tis easier. Give the prisoner a boost."

She took two steps, hopped up and caught a low-hanging bough. Then swinging her lithe legs in an arc, she swiveled over and around the branch to alight on the next limb. Her red braids dangled down at Warren like tempting tails of ivy. "Come on. There's plenty of footing."

Warren swallowed. Heights were never kind to him. Whether he'd visited the watch of a lord's fortress, scaled a mountain, or navigated the parapets of his father's castle, he'd usually found some way to circumvent the loftier heights that vexed him. His training included riding, fighting and archery, not this. But damn if he would let the wily redhead best him yet again.

Using his good arm, he grasped hold of the lowest bough and allowed the rough guard to give him a stirrup boost. Bracing his abdomen on the limb, he pulled his legs up and over. Now one more to go…

"That's it," she whispered. "Now, again." When he looked up, she was already on the next limb, her small body disappearing in the tangle of thick branches.

"*Bon sang!*" His shoulder ached deep inside where the climb had pulled his muscle. Holding the useless arm against his body, he glanced down. Sayer had already left to find his own hiding place.

He could not go any further. The sounds of horses crashing through the scrub made his pulse quicken.

The woman reached down for him. "This way. There are footholds, see? Even one of your kind can do it. You only need one good arm to hold on."

Devil wench! He *would* climb. He would do so to reach her and share his vexation!

He took hold of the branch she indicated and planted his boot on first one wobbling limb and then another two feet higher up, scaling the knotted tree branches until he came face to face with the princess. She clasped his arm and guided him into her hiding place, where he squatted down next to her to wait.

Four horsemen entered the clearing, their winded coursers scratched, bloody and angry.

To harm good horses for him? 'Twas abominable. He made a fist, barely controlling his anger. "Why are we hiding if you know him?"

"Shhh!" Her eyes widened in alarm.

Warren wasn't cruel to women and had never cared for those who were, but the way the fiery beauty's emotions transformed her intrigued him. He'd witnessed her fury (at him, mostly), as well as her curiosity (again, directed at him), and even a hint of her well-banked humor, but fear was new.

The riders made a slow circle of the clearing. One dismounted, and the finest dressed in the group pointed at the road.

Lord Vaughn. Keeping his voice at a whisper, he said, "If you won't answer my questions, methinks I'll address them to him."

Eleri's hand clutched his arm and squeezed. "You can't join them. They want nothing more than to watch you die." Her face was a hand's breadth away from his, her golden eyes luminous and her lips drawn with concern.

"To die now would be a mercy. Living as a slave..."

He made to stand, but she pulled him back.

"They would see you suffer!" Her fingers gripped him with all their might.

He covered her hand with his and enjoyed the reaction on her expression—a shifting blend of horror and a glimmer in her eyes from something altogether different. A chord of excitement ran through him.

"An answer for an answer, Princess. Who is he?"

"Your timing is poor. They'll hear!" she rasped.

Warren unfolded, but the woman tugged furiously at his arm as the men below continued to talk amongst themselves. He eased down again, closer than before so he could feel the warmth of her body. He inhaled the now-familiar scent of wildflowers in her hair.

She frowned. "All right! Lord Vaughn is...*was* my husband's cousin. He would also like to claim Dinefwr from Prince Lew, my brother-in-law. Now you." Her gaze flicked worriedly between the men below and him. "Why did you come here?"

Warren peered down. Armed and strong, these rebels would be difficult to overpower. The princess and her two attendants might be good with bows, but on foot or horse, he would wager on the newcomers.

"It no longer matters why I came to your country. You've killed all five of my men. Stephen of Blois…er, the *king* will retaliate."

"Five men?" she chirped, then covered her mouth in surprise. The wind rustled through the trees around them, carrying the sounds of their words away. In a lower voice, she continued, "You said this before, but there were *four* men. And you, of course."

Warren's stomach lurched. *One of the soldiers was alive?*

"What did you do with the bodies?" he demanded.

She winced, then regarded him gravely. "As was his duty, Lew ordered for them to be burned. We could hardly leave their corpses to be discovered by more invaders. Even though we are enemies, I am sorry we could not give them a Christian burial."

Her sympathy mattered not. They were six men against a Deheubarth army. "I wish you had not done so. Our conroi dispersed when you ambushed us. I cannot tell their families how or where—"

"Shhh…" One of the men below held up a hand, hushing the others. "Did you hear that?"

Eleri eased her bow off her shoulder and took an arrow from her quiver. Her arm formed a perfect line of sleek, appealing muscle as she aimed her barb at the lordling's back. Her eyes narrowed as she held her breath. Silent and unseen, she was as lethal as any knight Warren had ever seen in combat.

Nay, he'd been wrong before. He would wager on Eleri against these fools.

But if one of his men had lived and escaped, that changed everything.

He leaned forward, then pressed his lips against her ear. She trembled, causing him another dark thrill. "You may as well point that at me," he murmured. Her aim slipped minutely from her target while her muscles shook as she fought for control. "Tell me why you'd risk your neck to keep me from falling into this man's grasp or I'll cry out. Why should I care who rules your camp? Your Prince Lew slaughtered my men unfoundedly."

"'Twasn't Lew's fault," she hissed, "but I cannot explain. Not now!"

Taunting her, Warren hung over the side as if to yell, trying not to think of the height while keeping his gaze fixed on Eleri. Her eyes were no longer on her quarry but on him, reflecting venom and fear.

"Stop!" she whispered, relaxing her bow as she placed a soft hand over his mouth. Her eyes pleaded.

He peeled her fingers away and gripped her hand. Anger filled his chest. "Stop? For what price? You hope to beg a hefty bargain for my head? Or...mayhap trade me for support against this Lord Vaughn? Aye! That's it, isn't it?" He smiled coldly when her cheeks went whiter still.

"Stop! I *order* you to stop!" she rasped.

"Order?" he scoffed. "You're in no position to order me. What have you to trade for my silence?"

She frowned, her forehead glistening with light moisture in the moonlight. Seemingly vexed, she watched his lips—probably waiting for the first sign of his disobedience.

But if one of his men lived, he needed to return and find him, and if the princess would not help, he must escape immediately. He might be able to bargain with the rebels below. Surely they would be more sensible than this stubborn woman.

He opened his mouth to beckon the men, but Eleri moved like lightning. With her right arm restrained, she couldn't cut him. However, her weapon of choice caught him completely off-guard.

Her lips sealed to his, cutting off his voice in a hard kiss.

The astonishing action nearly toppled him from their roost, bold as it was, but he still held her hand. Bracing his back against the gnarled tree branches, he relaxed for more, but the kiss ended as briskly as it had begun.

The princess cupped her mouth with a trembling hand.

Beneath their tree, horse hooves churned through the dry leaves as Lord Vaughn and his men followed Nest's trail away from the camp, but Warren and Eleri remained frozen, their gazes locked.

Blood surging through his body, Warren grinned and lowered his face over hers. "Not the price I had in mind, but…um, shall we see what else you have to offer?"

Chapter Four

Sitting back on her heels, Eleri inhaled deeply from the breeze, letting the crisp, calming air soothe her warm skin. She pressed the back of her hand to her damp forehead, where the flush of mortification was still stamped on her flesh.

Oh Goddess! If only she could be as one with the tree around her, blending into the cold gray bark, melding into the forest, as camouflaged from the eyes of other men as she had been from her former husband.

More importantly, she wished to be hidden from the man looming inches above her with laughter in his gaze and a strong hand around hers.

She had no one to blame but herself. Trusting he would behave, she'd led him up the tree to hide. Then to cease his mutterings, she'd meant to distract him with a false offer. A kiss for his silence. What was she thinking?

Mayhap she'd thought that he would find a princess's boon—*along with saving his life*—reward enough. But like Vaughn, the Norman wanted more than what she was willing to pay.

Or...mayhap she'd thought she was strong enough to kiss him and retreat unscathed, but now her heart hammered against her ribs. His suggestive words and steamy gaze were no jests. This man was the enemy—not someone to play games with. Her lips still tingled from the scruff of his beard and the warmth of his mouth. *A fool was what she was!*

That mouth—De Tracy's mouth—softened as his mischievous smile melted and his gaze grew more determined. She felt his grip on her adjusting. He seemed to have forgotten his fear of the height. Not relinquishing his hold, his fingers curled around hers and his thumb swept the back of her hand, rough as a millstone yet light as a feather. "Your offer was not freely given, Princess?"

"'Twas no offer," she lied, lifting her chin. "Only a means to silence your tongue."

His eyes sparked with heat. "Only that and naught else? I think we should try and see what other sounds my tongue can produce. We'll both find pleasure in less talking."

His head lowered, shrouding her in shadow, and a sense of panic mixed with excitement took over her body. She flattened her hand against his chest and felt the steady beat of his heart beneath his tunic and the healer's bandaging.

Eleri took in another deep breath but instead of air this time all she found was the scent of the forest she'd created in his poultice, mint and all male. Her ears filled with buzzing, and her instincts urged her to draw closer to him, as well as to retreat. She turned her face away, and her blood hummed louder, working its warmth through her veins.

De Tracy's head brushed against her cheek in a caress of his soft unruly hair, and his breath touched her ear again the same as it had when she'd been armed, unable to move. Then, she'd been a frozen rabbit beneath the eye of the hawk, unable to defend herself. Now she could ward him off yet somehow chose not to.

His lips touched the soft place beside her earlobe in a slow gentle kiss. He murmured, "I would not take what you do not freely offer."

A shudder ran through her. She angled her head, hoping to catch his expression, but he blocked the moonlight. Steady as the hunting bird of his poem, he watched her, verily with more success than she, as the moonbeams at his back poked through the arms of the yew to illuminate every guilty thought on her face.

To her shame, she did wish for more, and disappointment in herself stoked her hot temper. "Good. Sayer would kill you if you tried."

The corner of his mouth curved. "Truly?" His bemused tone suggested he hadn't thought of that idea before. He caught one of her small braids between his thumb and forefinger and glided down its length before dropping the plait between her breasts.

"Aye," she said with a slight waver in her voice betraying her fear. Oh, she shouldn't have put another idea into his crafty head! Quickly, she added, "But you would suffer my blade first."

He chuckled. "Worry not. My death no longer appeals to me. You've given me something to live for."

His voice was somber, but his words gladdened her. She could not fathom why it pleased her so much knowing he no longer sought to die. He was her enemy. She'd done nothing to encourage him, nothing to assuage his guilt or suffering from the humiliation of his conroi's defeat.

Ah, but the fifth man…

"The one who lived, was he the one who put the arrow in you?" Intrigued by his mysterious injury, she traced the path of bandaging beneath his garment with unsteady fingers, stopping above the point of his wound. A few inches lower and to the left and the barb would've pierced bone, his lung or even his breastplate. He'd not worn the protective Norman mail. That fact had escaped her until now. Defenseless that day, he'd made an easy target.

Her question seemed to douse the mood that had held them in its spell. He released her and ran his hand down his face. "Of course not. One of *your kind* did this."

Eleri felt a squeeze of empathy in her middle, and she wrapped her arms around herself. Suddenly sad, she shook her head. "You are mistaken. I was with our archers—all of them except poor Iolo—in the treetops to the east. We did not shoot you, nor did we have any Norman barbs, which is what we dug out of you. Our arrows wouldn't have missed their target."

He sat back on his haunches and braced his hands on his knees. "*Il n'est pas possible*."

The sound of an owl brought their heads up.

"Sayer." She stood and moved to the opening in the tangled boughs where they'd entered. Leaning out, she returned his signal.

Her guard, friend and protector was closer than she'd suspected, but she prayed not close enough to see what had transpired between her and De Tracy.

A coil of rope dropped across the branches. Eleri wound the cord around one of the thicker boughs, and Sayer soon glided down to join them. His big arms draped across a branch as he faced them, his expression lost in the shadows.

"Are they all out of sight?" She rubbed the spot where her enemy had kissed her, convinced his touch had somehow left a visible mark in the darkness.

"Aye, but they weren't alone. Another rider followed at a distance. He turned off the path when they stopped and disappeared in the forest."

"One of Vaughn's or the prince's?" Eleri pulled her bow higher on her shoulder and looked into the gloom. A thread of unease ran through her that someone could be out there, watching unseen. Oak trees spread out endlessly into the night.

"Neither. He wore a domed helmet."

"Norman," she echoed with Warren de Tracy, and he glanced at her, frowning.

Not possible? She held her sarcasm to herself. He might be her enemy, but one of his own men had meant to kill him. Mayhap hunted him still. That idea festered in her like an open wound. The captive was hers! She'd taken him in the skirmish. No man, Norman or Cymreig, would steal the vengeance owed her, nor cause the wraith's prophecy to come true.

"Well, my lord is in a fine position." She sighed dramatically. His dark eyes lifted to hers. Remnants of anger and disbelief clouded his expression. "You are wanted dead by both your people and mine. You must have done something dreadful to deserve such."

He said nothing in return to argue or deny her accusation, merely backed into the shadows. Silent at last.

Day broke with the sounds of horses and voices. Warren recognized Sayer and Nest communicating in brisk tones, but when he pushed himself upright to see them, his legs and arms were restrained in two lengths of rope. New anxiety brought sweat to his brow upon the memory of the night before and how Princess Eleri had ordered him tied to the tree branches several feet from the safety of the ground.

After they'd traveled deeper into the forest that night, Warren had gleaned from the few details he knew of the territory that the River Wye was to the west and the Black Mountains were to the east. Sticking to the trees, his captors seemed to shun the easier territory of the barren hills where days of hiking could be turned into hours on the backs of the horses.

Warren gritted his teeth. Why bother with the coursers at all if they weren't going to ride them?

The rebels' concern over the Norman rider had to be unfounded. For all they knew, he could've been one of De Braose's sentries, making the evening rounds from the nearby castle. Warren had searched his memory for any clues that one of his conroi had wanted him dead and found nothing. If King Stephen had desired him gone, he'd have arranged it at court. An easy thing for him to accomplish with no need for subterfuge. A simple charge of treason and Warren would lose his head.

King Stephen had given Warren youthful knights for this quest—men striving to prove their loyalty to the new monarch, just like Warren. Stephen wasn't a popular choice as king, but he had more power in England than Empress Matilda. When Warren's younger sister Claire's future had been threatened with marriage to some lackwit distant cousin of the king's, Warren had made the difficult decision to pledge loyalty to Stephen—even though he detested the usurper.

Had his fealty angered one of Matilda's followers so much that the cur wanted him dead?

He'd drawn the ire of Henry's faithful before and had deserved it. His past was full of mistakes. If the murderer succeeded, Warren would accept his fate. He should have died years ago in the disaster at sea that took the true heir, Prince William's life.

Although, he reasoned, if he could locate De Braose's castle, he could salvage his mission by turning the tables on the princess and kidnapping her instead, taking her there. Then he would find out if the man Sayer had seen was a sentry or a would-be-killer, and the princess would have to face the consequences for the Deheubarth prince's actions.

But first, he had to get out of the damned tree and earn the trust of her pagan rebels.

He hailed them. "I pray you've not forgotten me."

His words were met by silence. As he'd feared, his attention to Eleri last night had caused her to regard him with more suspicion.

But tempted by her, he simply couldn't stop himself.

Cozied up against her soft form in their hiding place, his brain had become addled and his cock had taken control. After she'd brashly kissed him to keep him from shouting at Lord Vaughn, Warren had wanted to reciprocate with a kiss of his own...and more. The fact that she'd thought to silence him with her lips meant she'd at least thought about kissing him before that moment. He'd hoped to charm her into offering him another kiss—a lasting, deeper one which would lead to others—but apparently she'd read his intentions and would have none of him.

Should've just stolen the kiss. Should've parted her lips, caressed her tongue, given her all the pleasure she desired until she begged for release. Then you could've taken your own.

Warren strained against the ropes again. He must get down soon before his regrets became evident to his captors.

"Damn, I see you lived through the night." Sayer climbed onto the limb beside him. The branch bowed beneath his weight.

Warren grimaced. "No thanks to you. If one of our pursuers had returned to slaughter the three of you, I'd have been no help in this tree."

Sayer snorted. "You'd have been no help with half the Norman army at your back."

Warren bit back a retort. In his present condition, he could scarcely argue with the man. "I could be useful, though. Don't say you haven't considered the thought. You're all better archers, but I'm faster on the ground and on horseback."

Sayer grunted and stooped to untie him. "For a prisoner, you think highly of yourself. To arrive on foreign soil with no mail? The princess said you had the look of a noble son and spoke in Occitan. With your training you're no bard, no troubadour, nor priest. What are you? Templar? You're no monk, for certes!"

Warren was thankful the guard couldn't see the shock on his face. It had been two years since he'd worn the white mantle of the Order, and yet this Welshman recognized its stain on him.

He felt the ropes loosen on his arms as the man kept unwinding. Even under amicable circumstances, he never shared his past. The memory of his excommunication stung.

After Sayer took the rope away from his arms and legs, the man leaned back, studying Warren. "Your silence betrays you." His gruff voice and astuteness pricked at Warren's nerves, making him regret that he wasn't a skillful liar. "If it's a Templar you were, haps I should've left you tied up. An assassin with the blessing of the Church and his god…now that's a man with nothing to fear." Sayer's hand wrapped around the worn hilt of the sword in his scabbard, and his eyes narrowed.

Warren rubbed feeling back into his arms and squeezed his hands into fists. He returned the guard's stare. "As you said, I am no monk. Not then, not now. I am loyal to England, but that doesn't make us foes unless you choose to make it so."

Warren surveyed the Welshman. He was powerfully built and slightly older with gray at his temples. Whatever advantage in combat Warren had in speed, the rebel would overcome in experience.

Sayer gave him a faint nod, acknowledging his new understanding and, Warren hoped, an inkling of respect for his battle experience. "I'll remember to watch you more carefully."

Warren anchored an arm around a branch and peered down at the camp where Nest was stuffing a blanket into a bag on her horse's back. "Where is the princess?"

"At the river, not that it should matter to you."

Warren looked up from the dizzying view below. "Is that safe? What sort of guardian allows his princess to go about unprotected in woods with enemies afoot?" He frowned. This was far from the diplomacy he'd hoped to use with the man, but after years of combat, his instincts ofttimes overpowered his tact.

"The sort who follows the daughter of the King of Gwynedd. Besides, where she went, she had to go alone." Sayer's tone was defensive despite his assurances.

Still uneasy from the height, Warren sat, letting his legs dangle from the tree. His body prickled to life from the numbing sleep. "Surely her maid could've gone to attend her."

Sayer lifted a brow. "Nest? She's not a maid. She's a warrior, a shield maiden like the princess. Enough talk," he growled. "We need to keep moving."

As Sayer jumped to the next branch, leading the way to the ground, Warren's thoughts strayed to enticing images of Eleri bathing by the river. The water was too cold to swim, but he imagined her dipping a cloth, sponging her neck, and trails of icy water causing her nipples to peak.

Indeed he was no monk.

He compared Eleri against the women of his acquaintance in England. Elegant and refined, they complained of getting their slippers damp when they passed through the flower garden, and their fingers performed nothing more strenuous than stitchery. These rebel maids would seem built of iron by comparison if he hadn't been close enough to Eleri to know better. She was all soft skin and lean feminine muscle that his hands ached to stroke and explore.

Marrying her was thoroughly out of the question now after the Deheubarth attack, but seducing her was too tempting to resist. If she wielded half the passion in bed as she used in fighting, his efforts would be rewarded. Then he would bring her to the Norman keep—by force if he must. After all, hadn't she made him a prisoner first?

Chapter Five

Eleri pulled her fur mantle tight around her shoulders. The wind from the north swept through the mountains, penetrating the sanctuary of the valley passage, and her bliaut whipped against her legs. Soon they would visit hosts who would not approve of a woman wearing breeches, so she'd worn them beneath her gown, unseen yet still providing warmth and mobility.

With their enemies close, they had needed to change their plans by taking shelter during the day and traveling by night. She, Sayer and Nest walked their horses while the healing prisoner rode with his hands tied in case he chose to try and escape on horseback.

Eleri smothered a yawn in the sleeve of her gown as they trudged along the path. Her long vigils at the water's edge were beginning to take their toll. The *cyhyraeth* spirits had not returned for another death portent since Gwrach had wailed for Lew, but if there was going to be another Welsh death in either Deheubarth or her father's Gwynedd, Eleri would be the first to know.

Nest led the way and her long black braid swayed in time to her steps. Clever and loyal, the woman was the best friend Eleri could ever want. When they reached Gwynedd, she would have to ask her father to give both her guardians something in exchange for their faithfulness, though she already knew the two of them would ask for naught in return.

At the sight of a familiar flying rowan ahead, Nest lifted a hand, signaling the rest of them to stop. "A holy well lies around this hill."

Eleri sighed, relieved. "Aye. St. Anerin's Well. We should drink from it." She had noted the strain in Sayer's form and couldn't remember the last time he'd quenched his thirst. "Sayer will go first, and if the water is pure by his reckoning, we will follow." Her otherwise brave warrior avoided the rivers and streams with her at all costs, dreading he might see or hear the keening cries of the spirits.

As Sayer left the group and disappeared over the crop of boulders that spilled down from the hill, Eleri risked a glimpse at De Tracy. Her stomach fluttered to find him watching her. How long had he done so? Mayhap long enough to see how weary she was, and now he waited to take his chance to escape.

Reflexively, she reached for an arrow in her quiver and caressed the silken fletching. The corner of De Tracy's mouth curved, mocking her.

She hadn't meant the gesture as a threat, yet standing in the path of his cool, intelligent blue gaze, her control slipped piece by piece, as if by some ancient wizardry. Without saying a word to disconcert her, he had her second-guessing her movements, her motives.

Had she been concerned for Sayer's well-being when she'd called for water? For Nest? Or for Warren de Tracy?

Sayer reappeared and waved them closer. "The water is good." He raked the back of his hand across his dripping lips. "The hermit was wise to guard the place."

"St. Anerin?" De Tracy spoke to Sayer. "I've never heard the name of that particular hermit before. Is the well pagan or Christian?"

"'Tis water. Does it matter?" Eleri snapped, then glanced away. Her face heated. She sounded bitter like Vaughn. She softened her tone and fastened her bow and quiver to her horse's saddle. "No matter the deity, we could use the well's holy protection for our journey." She removed her sword from her saddle's pack and strapped it to her belt for the defense that only a proper weapon could offer.

"You'll not break any rules or anger God for sharing at this well," Sayer told the prisoner as he went to untie him. "St. Anerin was insane. Murdered by his own people. He wasn't called a martyr until many years later by those who knew him not."

De Tracy grunted and nodded his thanks. A new understanding seemed to have passed between them. Eleri did not care for it. Still, her anger had to cease. Railing at the captive for her own shortcomings was not the behavior of a woman of the royal Aberffraw family.

She handed him her drinking horn. "We'll make camp near a stream tonight, but 'tis hours away. Please...drink your fill."

De Tracy's hand covered hers on the vessel as he gently pushed it away. "You first, my princess. You're more tired than the rest of us. You keep the hours of the owl."

"Aye, and I hope my efforts are rewarded"—she forced a smile as she slid her fingers from beneath his—"by your health. Go and drink."

His steady eyes challenged her, not yielding.

She growled and snatched the horn.

After she scaled over the rocks out of his sight, new relief poured through her. The well sat in a vast alcove, peaceful and beckoning with stone steps inviting weary travelers, but the idea of the sanctuary didn't cause nearly as much solace as being away from the handsome knight.

Watching her footing and taking care not to fall on the slick rocks, she picked her way down toward the basin in the small amphitheater where the clear water pooled and mused on her own behavior.

She'd been angry when Owain had shunned their bed. Angry with herself for not being the woman he desired. His death had left many of her questions unanswered. For instance, why did she not please him? What had she done wrong, and would he have ever found her desirable again if he'd lived?

De Tracy stirred up those questions again. The first man to do so. His glances made her wonder if he found her attractive, or if he, like Owain, thought her simply a means of getting what he truly wanted. For Owain, marrying her had secured a powerful alliance with her father, but for the Norman, she held the key to his freedom.

And damn if he hadn't followed her to the sanctity of the holy well—if not in person, in her thoughts.

She crouched beside the water, scowling at her reflection as she dipped her horn into the drink.

"Allow me, Princess."

Eleri gave a start at the sound of her prisoner's voice, and she spun around to face him, sloshing all the icy water on her hand. "What are you doing here? Why did those two let you come alone?"

"They are having words. Something about sores from the ride." He grinned. "Rest while I get your water, *s'il vous plaît.* Besides, I've been sitting in the saddle all morning myself. I need to stretch."

She scanned the natural rock walls surrounding them, which prevented him from running. Her companions were talking in the distance out of sight. Rest sounded like heaven.

She gave him the vessel and wandered over to the stone seat. The cold from the rock permeated the layers of her clothes, and she shuddered.

De Tracy's eyes darkened as he returned with the water. "I've noticed you spend great lengths of time at the river and streams. Do you expect

Lord Vaughn to follow the tributaries?"

"Nay." She gulped down the sweet spring water and dried her mouth with her sleeve. She could tell him about her visions, but she didn't expect a Norman to understand. "Now you, my lord."

His lips tightened, but he took the empty horn and fetched a drink for himself. With his back turned to her, he used his right arm to draw the water with natural movements. Healing, he would very soon be a force to contend with for the three of them when he reached his full strength. She prayed they would hand him over to her father before such a time as he could wield a sword again.

Nest shouted from outside the alcove, her sound of alarm bouncing off the stones. Eleri stood just as a blur of black shoved her sideways, hurtling toward her prisoner. She fell to the floor and smacked her knee against the rock. Pain surged through her leg. Then, rolling onto her hip, she reached for her sword as Warren fended off the hooded assailant's blade with bare fists.

"De Tracy!"

She tossed her sword at him, hilt first. He caught it in his left hand in time to thwart the downward arc of the would-be killer's stroke.

Ignoring the biting pain in her knee, Eleri grabbed a loose rock and aimed at the attacker's back as De Tracy parried the man's blows in resounding clangs of metal.

The man's rabbit fur boots...the green mantle draped over the black hood...

Although she couldn't see his face, familiarity brought goose flesh to her skin and bile to her throat. She lowered her weapon as the two men fought, unable to make her shot as the two men turned, putting Warren's back to her.

Her prisoner was faster, stronger and taller, but the assailant struck him with the hilt of his sword against his bandaged wound.

Warren doubled over, wincing in pain, as his opponent lifted a sword high in the air for the killing blow.

Rampant fear seized inside her chest. She aimed the rock and caught the attacker in the side.

He yelped, dropped his sword arm and reached for the wound. She charged at him, but catching her progress, he rallied to retreat through the water for a hasty exit.

"Sayer! Nest!" She dropped her bow and slid an arm around Warren's back.

"I am not hurt." He leaned against her briefly, cradling his side, then righted himself, bracing against her shoulder gently for support. "I did not know him. Were you wounded?" He bent over her, struggling to catch his breath. Then, straightening, his hands swept down her arms, the bones of her hips, and skimmed her buttocks.

"No." She took a step backward, flushing.

His hand cupped her elbow and he drew her closer. "Are you? You were on the ground when I spied you."

She frowned, flattening her hands against his chest to keep a distance. His concern had her heart racing though the danger was gone. "He knocked me down. I didn't land well, but I'll be fine."

"*Bien*." He cupped her cheek with a gentle hand. His thumb brushed softly across her cheekbone, then passed over her lips. His gaze followed, focusing on her mouth.

Her breath caught with nervous anticipation.

"*Dywysoges*!" Sayer bellowed.

They moved apart. Regret engulfed her, and the dull pain returned to crawl up her leg.

The guard emerged through the rocks. "Are you two well? 'Twas the Norman again. He struck Nest down with a nasty blow to her right arm."

Eleri's gut clenched, and she forgot the throb in her knee. "There were two of them, then. How is she?"

"Madder than a fire-breathing dragon. The bastard realized his mistake when she hefted her blade in her left hand and chased him on foot." Sayer's gaze passed over her and then De Tracy, assessing the damage. "I take it our assassin's ally didn't fare well?"

Still favoring his side, De Tracy picked up the sword he'd used against the attacker and offered it to Eleri.

She touched the handle, then took her hand away. "Nay. Arm yourself."

His dark brows lifted with incredulity.

She touched her lips in thought, recalling the assailant's actions. "This was a planned attack to kill you. They watched us, waited until we were divided, then struck when they thought you were at your most defenseless. You should be able to defend yourself if you must."

Warren nodded. "But if Sayer's man was indeed Norman, who was the man you hit?" His eyes narrowed. "You knew him. You had the chance to hit him in the head, but you injured him instead."

Eleri bent her leg, testing it, and a new stab of pain made her grit her teeth. "'Twas Gareth, Owain's advisor. I know not how or why he tried to kill you, but I recognized him. And he wished that I had not."

When they rejoined Nest, she was leaning against her horse, rubbing her arm and swearing beneath her breath. "I hate Normans. I hate them all!"

Eleri gave her friend a hug and a kiss on the cheek.

Nest shrunk away, but flashed Eleri a brief smile before turning to mount her courser. "Now we simply must ride, Princess. If we continue to walk, we're easy targets. They wouldn't have gotten far."

Eleri touched Nest's boot before her distracted friend could ride away. "Gareth is with the Norman."

"Gareth?" Nest frowned.

"Aye. He attacked De Tracy. Lew might be in danger. I should've told him—"

Nest shook her head. "He wouldn't have allowed you to leave even if he'd known about the death portent."

"We must return to Castell Dinefwr at once and tell the prince what we've seen." Sayer went to retrieve his horse nearby.

Warren moved in front of Eleri, blocking her view of the others. She craned her neck to look into his serious eyes. "Princess, what if something has happened since we left? What if your enemies in Deheubarth have overthrown your Prince Lew? You could all be walking into a trap set by Lord Vaughn."

She shuddered, half in fear for her husband's brother and half in revulsion for the idea of bowing to Lord Vaughn. "You have a valid point." She moved around him and spoke to the others. "One of us will go back. The rest will continue on to my father's."

"I'll not leave you, Princess." Sayer's hands tightened on his reins.

"If you wish me to return, I will, my lady." Nest lifted her chin. "I can slip into the castell unnoticed and watch for the prince."

"He'll not be pleased with you," Sayer warned.

Eleri shook her head in disagreement. "I know my brother-in-law. He'll be angry at Nest, but more so with me. He would never blame her for something I've ordered her to do."

If her worst fear was true and something bad had happened to Lew, Gwrach would've let her know. And if he was in danger yet again, the wraith would cry for him that night.

As the last trails of sunlight faded from the woods surrounding their camp, Eleri left the men eating and returned to the stream they'd crossed an hour earlier. In a few moments, it would be dark, and she couldn't risk missing the death-portent, if there was one.

The stream, barely enough to hold a fish or two, bounced around a low, flat rock—a perfect place to rest and wait.

Gareth. Of all the people who would form an alliance with an enemy Norman, she'd never thought it would be her husband's confidant, his advisor and Lew's. They'd trusted him. Although they weren't on friendly terms, she'd had no suspicions about him in the past. Why had he suddenly come after De Tracy and in such secrecy?

Stewing over the day's events, she removed her boots, examining the worn places on the soles. She would never make it to Gwynedd in the old things. Mayhap she could buy more footwear from the white monks of the abbey.

A twig snapped behind her. She jumped up, palming her dagger instinctively. The sound had come from somewhere in the woods. Sayer wouldn't come near water when the *cyhyraeths* might appear, and he wouldn't allow De Tracy to wander off on his own. Someone else must be in the woods.

The assassins.

Without wasting time with her boots, she crept from the stream, pushing through bushes as quietly as possible. Thorns and broken acorns pierced the bottoms of her feet, but she pressed on in the direction of the sound. When she stepped out from the scrub, her mouth fell open at the sight of her prisoner on the back of one of their horses, making his way through the forest alone.

"De Tracy!"

He glanced over his shoulder at her cry, then galloped on as if he hadn't heard her.

She exhaled an angry breath. The scoundrel! Shoes or not, she had to get a horse and go after him before he was lost to them.

Running, she retraced her path back toward their camp.

Breathing hard, she didn't hear the telltale warnings until it was too late, running smack into the path of a wild boar.

As soon as she saw the massive bull, she froze. Standing statue-like, the beast fixed her with black, crazed eyes, his tusked mouth dripping with froth. He snorted and raked his hind legs menacingly.

She'd hunted boars before with the men. She knew sows protected their young with ferocity, but males were normally less aggressive. It made no sense why he would challenge her.

Still kicking, he made a slight turn sideways and she had the explanation. A hunter's spear hung from his side, spilling blood on the ground.

Her dagger would be useless. Too small, the blade wouldn't penetrate the wounded bull's hide enough to do any damage, and unfortunately, Sayer was too far away to call.

She looked up. The nearest tree branch was too high to jump for. Running was her only option.

She sheathed her dagger, readying for a sprint, then heard the sound of a horse and rider.

De Tracy's stolen black courser barreled straight for her. He leaned down from his saddle, holding out an arm for her. She reached for him and he scooped her up, depositing her facedown across his lap.

Awkwardly, she clung to him and the galloping horse while the ground passed under her, blurring inches from her dangling hair. At any moment she was sure to be violently sick, and De Tracy showed no signs of slowing down or stopping.

Had they not outrun the boar?

His hand remained around her ribs, gripping her securely. The sensation both comforted her and panicked her at once, with his warm reassuring touch lingering so near the swell of her bosom—which was presently pressed against his knee and the horse's shoulder. Her face heated as blood ran to her head. Worse still, her buttocks were pointed at her rescuer's face.

"My lord, you can stop now." She tapped his leg.

When he did nothing in return, she craned her head to see him. His expression was stoic and determined.

They were headed away from the camp.

"Merlin's beard! You're not going to let me go?" Slipping, she clutched his thigh and his muscle flinched beneath her touch.

His gripping hand inched higher, anchoring her with a hold that now cradled against her breast.

Sweat sprang to her brow even as her heart skittered with delight.

Kidnapped. Held at the mercy of this enemy. What would become of her? What would he *do* to her?

Nay. A thousand times nay. The Princess of Deheubarth would not allow herself to be captured by a Norman. She would rather die.

She pulled her dagger free and lifted it to make her intention clear.

De Tracy let go and reached for the blade. But she thrust backward to tumble off the horse. She dropped the dagger as she fell, landing on her side.

Winded, she rolled on her back and watched as stars filled her vision.

She lay there focusing on the treetops overhead, thanking the goddess she still lived. The fall had been hard, but she'd had worse.

"*Par le sang Dieu.* Are you mad?"

De Tracy appeared above her, breathing raggedly. His face was tight with anger as he looked her over.

She pushed up on an elbow, gasping for air, prepared to fight, but he dropped to his knees, putting a gentle hand on her shoulder.

"Are you hurt?" His hand went to the back of her head, feeling her scalp as he searched her arm for broken bones.

Again, his concern flustered her. She shook her head, dizzy, though not from the fall. She flattened her hand against his chest and stared into his eyes, too unsure of herself to speak. He'd saved her life and immediately afterward tried to kidnap her. At such a time, gratitude *must* be wrong.

He waited for an answer, so she gave him the first one she could. "Your hand…is in my hair again."

A tiny smile played across his lips. "*Oui.*" His fingers moved against her scalp, but he didn't release her. Instead, he lowered his face, stopping just inches above hers. "*Mon dieu.* I cannot leave without tasting your lips once more."

She read the question in his hooded gaze. She would not let him leave, of course, but allowing him a kiss seemed a reasonable consolation after saving her life. Especially as she wanted it, too. *Longed* for it.

She put her hand behind his neck, mimicking him, and threaded her fingers through his thick, wavy hair. "Take your kiss, my lord."

His lips touched hers softly as he brought her upright. She braced her other hand on his chest, and his heart raced beneath her palm. The kiss was chaste and brief. His mouth lifted, then floated to return two times, then three, then four. Each kiss left her lighter and lighter, becoming weightless, as if she were a feather drifting in the air.

The fifth time his mouth stayed upon hers, and his hand moved from her arm to her neck. Coarse fingers ran across the skin of her throat as if its texture pleased him, and indeed his touch pleased her, putting a fire low in her belly. His lips parted under hers and tugged gently upon her bottom lip, begging permission, which she granted, opening her mouth to him.

Cupping her jaw in his hand, he angled his head and moved inside. His tongue sought hers, caressing her with a long sweep. He tasted of the wine from dinner, rich and delicious.

She leaned against him, thirsting for more.

He continued to kiss her, his mouth becoming brash, seeking. He deepened the kiss, his tongue probing the inside of her mouth, his hands exploring her body, fingers splaying against her curves. New yearning filled her.

He drew away after a length, sighing, and plucked a leaf from her hair. "I am glad I returned," he said in a husky voice. His smoldering gaze moved uncertainly from her mouth to her eyes and back, as if trying to decide his next course of action.

Eleri trembled. She touched her mouth, and her lips were scalding hot. Never had she been kissed with such recklessness, such desire. Her hand dropped to his chest. She would have more…

Reading her thoughts, he placed a gentle finger against her lips, regarding her mouth with longing. "Your man will be coming at any moment. I left while he went to urinate."

Before she could find her senses and speak, he slid his arms around her and lifted her against him as he rose.

"What are you doing, Norman?" She wrapped her arms around his neck, though he seemed more than capable of carrying her without her help.

Suddenly, being weaponless in the knight's embrace seemed more precarious than traversing any treetops of her memory. Yet although her head protested, her body reveled in the sensation of his hard warm chest and secure arms.

"You will call me Warren," he corrected gently, "and I am putting you on the back of Bane—*my* horse, given to me by the Count of Anjou. I'm taking you to the keep of De Braose, Lord of Bramber. There you'll tell him what you know of this Gareth, and I'll tell him about the traitor amongst my men. I'm sure I have the two of them to thank for the ambush and the deaths of my innocent soldiers."

"Oh no. I'm not going to any Norman castell with you." Eleri kicked her feet to be let down, but he drew her tighter against the wall of his chest. His determined footsteps brought them closer to his stolen horse. *Not again.* "Put me down, Warren! Why should I help you?"

"Because—where are your boots, Eleri?" He had lowered her to the ground beside the horse, then noting her toes peeking out from under her skirt, swept her up again. "Because it would be in your best interest to appeal to the king. 'Tis for you I've come to Wales."

"For *me*?"

He lifted her to sit sidesaddle, grimacing in the action. "*Oui.*" He took hold of the reins and paused to give the horse's neck a rub, before continuing, "If it still pleases my liege, you will wed me there and—"

"Wed you?" Her heart kicked against her ribs, and she gripped the saddle, fearing she might fall. "You're mad! Why would I ever consent to marry you?"

His jaw tightened, and his eyes grew serious. "Because the King of England has ordered it."

Chapter Six

Warren knew women as he knew his own sword, from one end to the other, as well as how to please them, and he instantly recognized when he'd done or said something to cause their pleasure to cease. The fiery princess, who moments ago had fed his desire with a kiss so provocative he'd wanted to lose himself deep within her heat, was now an ice maiden. Spine arrow-straight and her head tipped up, she stared directly ahead as if she hadn't heard him announce his liege's plans for their betrothal.

Taking hold of his horse's bridle to lead, his arm brushed Eleri's leg. She flinched at his touch, drawing into herself with a shudder that mortified him more than he wanted to admit.

At least she wasn't trying to flee or fight again. He wasn't sure which would've been worse since his shoulder still burned inside and out from the assassin's attack at the well.

"So this is truly why you and your men were in Cantref Mawr when we ambushed you?" Her voice was small, less sure. She folded her hands in her lap.

He studied the side of her face, the way she'd tucked her mussed hair behind her ear and draped the cascading plaits over one shoulder, leaving the column of her creamy neck exposed, beckoning him for a nibble.

His tongue felt thick. "Aye. The king wishes to re-establish English authority over Deheubarth, as well as the other Welsh principalities, starting with Castle Dinefwr."

She turned halfway toward him, her eyes reflecting remorse. "'Tis too late now, but I want you to know we were told there were many more of you—an army—which we'd assumed was equipped for invasion."

The confession, delivered with such humility from the princess, nearly knocked him off his feet.

"You may rest assured, Eleri, I'll include this in my report to the king. I'll hold you blameless. Your leader..." He let her imagination finish for him. She'd shown great concern for her brother-in-law. He didn't want to alarm her when he didn't know what would happen either.

Despite her obvious discomfiture, her face remained luminous, almost ethereal. It made sense she'd been wed to the late Prince Owain, the ruler of a powerful territory. Coming from a royal lineage, she would've been considered a prize among men, and with rare beauty to boot, as well as a body a man would give anything to possess and enjoy night after night...

Of course she'd made a good match, but to Warren's reckoning, her intelligence made her more of an equal. No wonder she fought as she did alongside them.

Blood quickened to his groin.

He needed a second horse for Eleri. At the moment, he couldn't possibly share Bane with her, enduring a ride with his rigid flesh against her perfect buttocks. He forced himself to think of less pleasant things than the beguiling woman—his mother, for one, who wore an expression similar to Eleri's when vexed with one of her lovers.

"Lew is more boy than man, still learning from his mistakes. Even so," her eyes gleamed down at him with renewed mischief, "you don't know where De Braose's keep is, and I won't tell you."

The more she challenged him, the more he wished to spar…though not with words.

"Then we'll wander aimlessly until we find it." Desire made his voice hoarse.

Eleri's brows lowered. "That isn't a wise idea. Did you happen to see the boar back there? Did you get a good look at it?"

A smile tugged at his mouth. "Terrifying."

She exhaled, scowling. "If you saw the beast, then you must've seen the spear in its side."

"Aye. What of it?"

"A huntsman's spear. Possibly an Englishman's, but more likely a local clansman's. He would be stalking his kill, waiting for the creature to bleed to death. And he would be hunting with other men."

Her voice sounded smug. He stopped their progress to give her his full attention. "And if we cross paths with this hunter and his clan?"

She grinned coolly. "Sayer and I will share in the kill with wine at the table of our neighbors, but as for you…" She clucked her tongue and shook her head, feigning sadness.

Bane's head tugged against his hold, ready to keep moving, but Warren resisted. His face heated with indignation at her veiled warning. When he'd left England with his orders, he'd never expected his offer of a union sanctioned by the king to be met with a threat.

Yet even as her affront ruffled his pride, it failed to stop his lustful craving. Unfortunately, if he acted upon his urges now, dragging her from the horse and taking her into his arms again, she would surely reject him.

He gritted his teeth. "I find the risk preferable to life as your father's slave."

"Either way, the choice is yours, but do not expect me to go with you willingly." Her eyes darkened with challenge.

He needed her account of the chain of events to lend truth to his own. His past followed him everywhere. Try as he might, no deed ever seemed to rectify the damage he'd done. If the princess chose to cry foul against him and claimed he'd threatened her people, King Stephen would accuse Warren of disobedience—or worse, treason.

He required her allegiance.

Gathering all the strength he possessed, he kept his boiling emotions in check. "What would you have me do? These hunters may be upon us at any moment, as you say. If we return to camp and they find us there, do you intend to send me back into the treetops to hide?" Although the rebels depended upon the trees for defense, the tactic seemed cowardly by comparison to the ways of his brave Templar and Norman brothers-in-arms.

She watched him seriously for a moment, finding something of interest in his response. Then she shook her head. "We have another day of travel before we take shelter. I had already planned to hide you, though not in the trees." She swiveled back around, preparing to ride. "Take me back to the stream for my boots, then I'll explain."

Warren weighed his options. Armed with his sword again, he felt freedom beckon, but at what price? Another accusation of treason, or death at the hands of some barbaric tribe? He would bide his time with Eleri a little longer.

Retracing their path, Warren led Bane back to where he'd first seen her as she'd spotted him attempting to escape. He should've known he couldn't make his exit quietly enough. In Devon, he'd hunted en masse with his brother and friends, so stealth had never been necessary for their sport. Then in the Holy Land, he'd hunted with falcons—again he'd had no need to temper the noise of his horse. No wonder the princess, herself a half-fey creature, had caught him trying to flee.

Admit it. You wanted her to catch you. Wanted that last taste of her.

He would have more than a sample of her lips when he took her to the castle.

When Eleri moved to dismount, Warren stopped her, putting a hand on her knee. "Nay, you're barefoot. I'll fetch your boots." He sighed and handed her the reins, avoiding her gaze and whatever objection she might raise.

He turned and plunged into the brush, taking the direction he'd seen her come from.

The thorny bramble opened to more woods. He startled a ground-dwelling bird, whose beating wings sent a burst of surprise through him, too. No wonder the princess thought him an ill choice for bridegroom. He could not perform such a simple task as walking through the forest without disturbing the tranquility.

He rubbed his sore shoulder as the stream appeared in the clearing. Eleri's boots lay beside a stone where she'd no doubt sat to remove them. What was she doing bathing in such cold weather? He crouched to pick them up, surveying the area for anything else she might've left when he'd interrupted her.

Movement downstream caught his attention.

A hunchbacked and bedraggled old woman appeared at the side of the water. Alone, she limped clumsily forward, not having seen him. Perhaps she was one of the huntsman's tribe.

He rose slowly with Eleri's shoes in his hands, searching the trees for any signs of the woman's companions, but saw no one.

The old woman waded into the water. *Bon sang*, she was naught but skin and bones. A more revolting creature he'd never seen, with fingers like bird's claws and a shriveled face. She began washing her hands.

"*Fy ngŵr, fy ngŵr!*" she wept over the splashing water.

Warren's stomach squeezed at the pathetic sight. He should offer her some form of aid. He followed the stream, looking for a place where he could ford and approach her. She might be in pain. He knew nothing about herbs and medicine but Eleri seemed somewhat knowledgeable in healing.

When he was directly across from her, she turned about and made for the bank.

"Are you hurt?" he asked.

Her cries died away, and she drifted toward the woods she'd come from as if she hadn't heard him. He shrugged and went back. There was no time to follow her. Eleri was waiting, and the boar was still loose. A flash of light came from behind him. He glanced over his shoulder, and the harpy was gone. *Strange*.

The hair stood on his arms. He searched the darkening sky for signs of a brewing storm, something to explain the brilliant flash of light, but there was nothing except a clear sky and stars overhead. Mayhap his wound had begun to fester, and now his mind played tricks on him.

When he reached Eleri still sitting atop Bane, she studied him as he handed up her boots. "What's wrong?"

Better to keep silent than admit to her he'd seen a deaf woman whose horrible visage sent a chill through him more troubling than the assassins and her maddened boar combined.

He relaxed his brow and shook his head. "Nothing of importance."

Later that evening, Sayer snared three rabbits for supper, and the meat sat heavy in Warren's stomach as they rested by the campfire. The guard tipped back his drinking horn, gulping noisily.

As much as Warren liked Sayer, he disapproved of the man's drinking and the risk to the princess's safety. Eleri hadn't told her friend that Warren had attempted escape, but he had yet to figure out why. Pride, mayhap, but was it her own? Or out of respect for the guard's?

The princess kept watch over a boiling pot and poured its steamy contents into a bowl. Having shed her bliaut, she now wore breeches and a linen tunic, which displayed her lean curves as she rose and walked in the shadows. When she disappeared into the woods and blessedly out of his field of vision, he felt as if he'd been released from a spell.

Celibacy had been one of the first oaths he'd broken upon quitting the Order, but he'd not been with a woman since he'd last visited court.

"Why did you become a Templar if you didn't want to take orders?"

Warren's gaze cut to Sayer's and feeling his glare, his neck heated. "A penance, I suppose." He shrugged, unwilling to explain his regret to the Welshman, no matter how forthright he felt in the warrior's company. Instead, he continued, "My life was worth nothing. I had no property, no title. Other noble sons had done the same. It was the only thing for a man in my situation to do. Still is, though the Templars were not as altruistic as I'd expected." In fact, he hated the memory of the so-called holy wars he'd fought in that land—the greed behind the ordered slaughter of a people.

Sayer grunted. He stretched out on his sleeping mat and braced his head on an elbow. His eyes looked heavy, and rightly so. He'd drained the last of the wine from dinner.

Eleri entered the camp again, coming from the opposite side of the fire with fur pelts in her arms she'd taken from the satchels on the horses.

An owl suddenly fled a tree branch above them, making a startled whoop. The princess gasped, putting a hand to her heart. Then turning to meet Sayer's gaze, she smiled broadly, laughing at herself—a lovely, unaffected grin which Warren longed to receive.

She threw a fur blanket in Sayer's face when he laughed too.

Warren burned with envy.

The guard drew the cover over himself and rolled onto his side. His snores followed almost immediately.

Left alone with Eleri, Warren's mind reverted back to where it had been a moment ago, to her tempting curves, her soft skin and fluid movements. She picked up the cooling vessel by the fire and strode toward him.

Sitting upright, he clutched his gut. "Nay. I'm full."

Her eyes glittered with mirth. "'Tis not food. Remove your shirt, and I'll show you."

If she'd wanted to make overtures of a sexual nature, she wouldn't do so in front of her guard, sleeping or not. Warren had no such qualms himself.

He doffed his tunic to put behind him.

She dropped to her knees in front of him, staring at his shoulder with concern. "I've brought you a different medicine. Father's warriors swear it helps them heal faster for battles. There's bruising where Gareth hit you, but the bastard didn't reopen the wound. 'Tis a blessing and a wonder he didn't." She passed him the bowl. "'Tis still a little hot, but that's when it works best. Rub it around the cut."

The liquid was dark and smelled of pungent pine. "What are you about, Eleri?" He thrust the bowl at her.

She rocked back on her heels, refusing to take it. "Trust me. This is the answer to your healing until we reach the safety of the abbey."

He raised an eyebrow at her. "What is this sudden concern for my well-being?"

Her eyes flashed, but she smiled wryly. "You have nothing to lose if it doesn't work…unless your Templar oaths forbid you from using pagan medicines…"

"So you heard?" He glanced at Sayer's back, his body motionless and snoring beneath his blanket. Returning his gaze to Eleri, his cheeks heated. She would've found out sooner or later, but her knowledge of his shameful past stung. "I don't know what you've heard about Templars, but I've broken most of my oaths. I've severed my ties with their murderous kind. God has worse quarrels with me than what I do to myself." He looked away, avoiding those sharp eyes.

"Good. Do it then, and I'll plait your hair as Sayer wears his. 'Tis better to smell and look like one of our kind than Norman."

Without waiting for his consent, she hopped up and came to sit beside him.

The instant her hands fell on his head, his objections died on his tongue. Not that he cared how he might look with the tiny plaits the Deheubarth wore to keep their hair out of their eyes—and he'd long outgrown the round-topped cut of his brethren Templars—but the braids seemed the very embodiment of a rebellious, untamed culture. That added to the strong-smelling ointment and he would be exactly as she'd said. Deheubarth.

Now who's proud?

If his pride didn't kill him, her close presence would.

He slapped the oily salve upon his wound, relishing in the burn. The effect failed to pull his attention from the lovely redhead whose dexterous fingers worked in his hair and whose soft, full breasts rubbed his shoulder as she wove the strands. From her kneeling position, the hollow of her throat stood before his eyes, smooth skin beckoning for his exploration. Forgetting the bowl, his task, and everything around him, he reached for her. Sliding his hand around her alluring neck, he held her still.

"Warren—" Her eyes widened as she drew in a breath. She stiffened but did nothing to resist, nothing to contest him. Her chest rose and fell as she stared back at him, and her lips parted, exposing the glimmer of her tongue within, the beckoning of invitation.

But he would taste her skin first.

He leaned forward and buried his face beneath her chin, darting his tongue to the very spot that had been the focus of his attention these past few days. He licked the concave softness, relishing the vulnerable point—perhaps one of the few the brash young woman possessed.

Her hands dropped on his shoulders, and she whimpered.

Yearning overcame him, making him want to explore every inch of her body for more such places. He would not stop until he conquered them all.

Desire slammed through Eleri. Warren's lips and tongue swept along the crevices of her neck, while his thumb passed up and down. Her heart beat like the feet of an ensnared hare. Panicked, she backed away to restore her pulse.

"Don't do that," she whispered. "Sayer—"

He peered over her shoulder briefly then reached for her again. "If we're quiet, he'll sleep well past dawn."

She pulled from his hands even as waves of unearthly pleasure sprouted beneath his touch. "'Tis very wrong, and you know it. Let's finish."

His hungry gaze followed her as she moved to his other side. This time she kept more distance between them, stretching from afar to braid his hair.

He changed positions, his jaw clenching, but dabbed his fingers in the concoction without objection.

Idle conversation would surely help ease the tension between them. "Your hair is quite long, my lord." She selected three small strands and set to work.

He rubbed the tincture in a circle around his wound. "My sister offered to shave my head, but I've found the length keeps the sun off. Helps cushion my helmet too."

"You have a sister?" She imagined his eyes and hair on a beautiful young lady.

"And a half-brother, Dom. My sister Claire is ten." He wrinkled his nose. "I'm sure she meant well, but even if I wanted my hair short, I would not ask her. She cannot sit still for a moment. My brother and I took her fox hunting once. We came back with naught but saddle sores from trying to keep up with her palfrey and thorns in our legs from when she decided to chase a rabbit into the thicket instead."

Eleri laughed, and he smiled. Sharing in the warmth of his story put a different sort of flame inside her. She eased behind him, starting a braid where she wouldn't be tempted to stare into his dancing eyes.

He cleared his throat. "I have the wound covered, methinks. Verily, I will be green for days."

"You've barely put it on at all. There's still more in the bowl." She smiled. Despite her better judgment, she crawled in front of him to wet her fingers in the bowl.

His skin glistened with the verdant color, making a perfect canvas she longed to fill.

Unable to stop herself, she put her moistened fingertip just beneath the cleft of his chin and made a curved line, creating a swirl around his neck. She repeated the stroke an inch lower. His skin was warm and smooth—a pleasure to touch—his chest rising and falling beneath her ministrations like a majestic warlord of old. She fell under a trance, certain she would be content to touch him thusly all day and night.

The next time she pulled away to re-moisten her fingers, Warren's hand dropped on her thigh. Innocent enough…until she leaned over to trace a pattern beneath his neck and into the valley of his muscled chest. His thumb rubbed intimately across her pelvic bone, and his breath rushed out, stirring her hair. She met his gaze and found him watching her with a predatory look.

He might've been full, but wasn't sated. His transparent hunger filled her with excitement.

He leaned forward slowly and took her willing lips. She opened her mouth and his tongue slid inside.

He built a rhythm with each stroke of his tongue, while his hand came to hold her side, just beneath her breast. She relaxed her tongue against his, savoring the expertise of the kiss and the sinful pleasure of his hand on her body. His touch was everything she knew she should not abide, and yet everything she craved. His fingers fanned across her breast, and she heard a sound escape her throat, only to be swallowed by his kiss. If he could make the rest of her body sing as well…

She shifted, giving him more of her breast for his exquisite handling. Vaguely she felt his movement as he set aside the medicine, and then his other hand flattened against the small of her back while he pushed deeper into her mouth. Guided by his actions, she leaned against him, wanting more, needing to feel his skin.

His hand eased down the slope of her back, cupping her buttocks. Gripping her, he moved back, pulling her atop him before he leaned on his elbows. The juncture of her thighs touched the hardened staff between his legs, and she jerked away in alarm.

"Warren—"

He put his finger against his lips, silencing her. Then, he settled back on the fur beside her. "Finish your healing. I won't touch you, if you don't want me to." He slid his left hand into his breeches. Stroking himself slowly, back and forth, his gaze held hers.

Her heart jumped in her throat. She had caught her husband giving himself relief in such manner when he thought no one was around, but he'd never done so with the intention of her seeing.

For Warren to do so here? In her presence?

Ignore him!

He withdrew his hand to take hers and pulled it close until the turgid flesh beneath the material filled her palm. "You're driving me mad. You see? 'Tis all I can do—" he broke off, swallowing.

She glanced back at Sayer. Still sleeping. Then she looked upon Warren's face, his expression tight in the firelight. Light and shadows danced over his muscled form as he made himself more comfortable. Her unguent on his tan skin made him look primeval, raw and strong in the flickering firelight.

She yanked her hand from his, curling her fingers into her palm. To cover her lack of experience, she feigned interest in his scar and the taut muscle running over his chest, rippling over arms marked with other intriguing pale scars from long past. His motions drew her attention, however, as he stroked his flat stomach.

Fascinating. Perspiration beaded on her upper lip. She told herself it was the fire, but the real heat was coming from the man lying next to her.

Putting one arm behind his head as a pillow, he angled himself to watch her, leering as if he'd heard her thoughts as he continued to touch himself.

She dragged the bowl closer with a shaking hand and trembled as she applied the mixture in another swirl against his collarbone.

"Like what you see, Princess?" He laughed breathlessly.

Aye, she longed to respond, but the scoundrel needn't hear it from her lips.

"You tease me," she accused in a tiny voice.

She took another dab of herbs and reached for his stomach, but his rough grunt stopped her.

"Move your hair off your shoulder," he rasped.

Her gaze shot to his, and she found him snarling, his eyes hooded. He slid his hands beneath his waistline and pushed the fabric down his lean hips until his organ appeared, long and engorged.

Her hand shook as she did as he instructed, exposing her neck to him as she strained to keep her eyes fixed on his face and the upper half of his body. She didn't want to think about the way he held himself, working as he admired her.

"Your skin is so pale against your hair. Beautiful. I imagine your thighs are, too, against your curls."

Her breath caught at the candid remark, and she swayed mid-reach for him. Her legs parted in the movement, drawing his gaze.

He made a strangled sound in his throat. "I would chafe you there with my teeth. I'd like to see your skin flush. I'd chase it with kisses, then watch your eyes drift closed."

She held her breath. Aware she'd allowed her eyes to do just that, she forced them open.

He bit his bottom lip. Then his knees bent and his hips canted. His hand followed his now-glistening cock to the dark hair at the base, and he groaned with his broad stroke.

"The way you're looking at me, Eleri… One word from you, and I'll haul you into the woods right now."

Her gaze descended along his glistening torso as her stomach somersaulted. He was perfection, and he wanted her. She could have him with a word…

Guilt licked her cheeks as she sat frozen in indecision. Searching for something chiding to say instead, she moistened her lips, and Warren responded with a low growl that vibrated a chord deep inside her—a note of pleasure she wished he'd pluck again.

He panted, "Tonight, before you sleep, touch yourself and think of me and what I long to do to you."

Her inner thighs ached at his suggestion, keening for fulfillment. Dare she do as he said? She wanted to. *Damn him!*

His gaze locked with hers, dark as night and as unreadable as the man's soul. Hard and fast, he convulsed with the explosion of his spilling seed, the final lash striping across his stomach.

She rose unsteadily, for the first time not brave enough to meet his eyes. Her shaky thighs felt damp with her own unrequited need as she made her bed on the opposite side of the fire. Mayhap that had been his intention all along—a cruel trick on his captor—making her lust when he knew she could not ease herself. It was almost as if he knew what she'd been denied in the marriage bed—passion—and he could so obviously provide it for whomever he wed.

But he was her enemy, was he not?

Whatever the cost, she *must* avoid touching him until they reached their destination.

She spread out a blanket and in doing so, glanced at the front of her tunic. A green handprint fanned across her breast, where the echo of its owner's weight branded her again.

Chapter Seven

When the tidy stone walls and rooftop of the monastery appeared on the horizon, Eleri noticed that Warren's shoulders relaxed, in contrast to Sayer, who exchanged a tense look with her. They had visited Bodin Abbey two years before when she had first moved south from her homeland with her betrothed, along with Nest. Now her friend rode ahead to greet the abbot's gatekeeper and let the monks know they were travelers from Deheubarth and not a band of brigands come to plunder.

Sayer would also inquire about Lord Vaughn or Gareth, in case they'd arrived ahead of them. She prayed their foes were long gone.

She had already washed and combed her braids out, and had donned her feminine bliaut beneath her cloak, making herself as Christian as she could in case they met any monks along the road. Gerald de Gernon, the abbot, disapproved of the ancient ways of the Cymry, but he found her reputation for ethereal visions even more repugnant. His welcome wouldn't be warm.

Upon seeing Sayer's wave to them, Eleri and Warren drew closer to the gate. She became aware of Warren's horse lagging behind her—the first time she'd been alone in the man's presence since their intimacy the night before. She hadn't been able to sleep, recalling what she'd witnessed, remembering the ecstasy of his kisses on her skin and his comment about what he wanted to do with her.

Madness. If she'd only been of her right mind, she would've scolded him for his actions, or at least left him alone to his pleasures. But she hadn't. She'd been too enraptured by his release, too spellbound. And now she only wanted to experience more.

"Princess," he hissed suddenly, his voice cool behind her, sending a quiver down her back. "You said we would be staying at an abbey, but you didn't say whether it was Welsh or not."

"Does it matter, my lord?" She kept her gaze fixed ahead.

"Aye. It does if it's Norman. Tell me this is not a French order."

The solemn architecture became more apparent as they approached the four stone buildings behind the wall. Romanesque with arched entries, the abbey was a far cry from the crude tribal fortresses and wooden buildings at Castell Dinefwr and the Glamorgan coast.

"I would think you'd be glad to see a familiar Savigniac house." She watched him from the corner of her eye.

He stiffened, his hands tightening on the reins. "You mean to hide my identity amongst French monks?"

Eleri smiled to cover her trepidation. Mayhap she'd gone too far this time. Mayhap he would turn on them.

She allowed herself another glimpse of the man. Pride and righteous anger hardened his expression. Beneath his unshaven chin, he wore a layer of pagan medicine running down his neck to disappear beneath Sayer's borrowed tunic. That, along with the braids in his hair, seemed a waving emblem of Welsh dissonance and rebellion against all things Christian, Norman and civilized. She'd marked him as the enemy of the Church, and now the wary brothers would doubt him if he claimed otherwise.

She prayed he would not retaliate with violence. Not only would he be a difficult adversary, but she also didn't wish to kill him. They'd saved each other's lives, after all.

"You forgot one thing." He smirked.

"I did?" Her brows went up.

"When I speak, they'll know I'm not your kind."

She mirrored his aloof expression. "Oh, but you won't speak. You're my captive. Know your place, Warren. We'll say you're a mute."

After a pause, considering, he finally nodded. "If I cannot speak to them, I also cannot speak to you. So be it. But…I'll need another name. You cannot call me Warren de Tracy." He glanced at the white-robed priest at the gate, and his eyes narrowed.

Eleri rubbed her temple where a headache had begun. He had agreed too readily. He didn't *want* to be recognized. Being an excommunicated Templar would make him ashamed, of course, but she felt it was more. Something else made him hide from these countrymen.

What if it had something to do with his assassin? Might the monks also consider him an enemy of the crown?

She would have to make inquiries later.

"Your name will be Yorath. You were shot fighting the Normans."

He didn't agree or disagree.

She added a serious note to her voice. "If you attempt to ask for help from the monks, Sayer and I will be forced to remove you from here, and they are…*unarmed*."

"You would shed their blood? I think not, Eleri. You're not cruel." He smiled. "Still, I'll pretend as you wish. 'Twill be a pleasure watching you handle yourself amongst other foreigners. No matter how uncomfortable you might find the clothes you're wearing now, you look more presentable. Almost like a woman."

She frowned, but refused to take his bait. "Unlike your army, these monks are here by invitation under a charter of good terms. They're not invaders. And they're certainly not trying to subdue my countrymen by killing our husbands and marrying our widows."

She dismounted and straightened her clothing as Abbot Gerald strolled across the lawn toward her with Sayer at his elbow.

Warren leaned down and captured her shoulder beneath his gloved hand. Startled by his sudden touch and the current of warmth his strength sent coursing through her, she glanced up with a gasp.

He whispered, "That's not my intention either. I'm not your enemy, Eleri."

Releasing her, he swung down from Bane in one graceful swoop, while Abbot Gerald extended a hand to her. The priest's eyes widened a fraction upon seeing the tall, unfamiliar Deheubarth warrior close behind her, but he quickly recovered, welcoming her with a practiced expression.

The travelers were ushered into the courtyard where monks took the horses to be fed and watered. Then the party was divided. Warren was taken to his berth in the stables—far from the skittish monks—while she and Sayer were told to follow Brother Allard to sleeping accommodations in the cells before supper later that evening.

Unease filled her at leaving Warren. These were his people, and he could still ask for their help. If not in protection, perhaps in aiding his escape. It would only take one monk to lead him to the Norman castle he sought.

But Warren had shown he wasn't willing to go there without her. He'd been ordered by his ruler to marry her. *Stupid, arrogant king!* And if he returned empty-handed, without his men, he would be humiliated.

So he stayed for her.

But what did he hope to accomplish? Surely he didn't expect she would swoon at his touch and accept his marriage troth.

Not her enemy? Nay, but she still felt unsettled in his company.

At last, left alone by the monks as she and Sayer stood outside the wooden doors of their rooms, Eleri dropped her cloak's hood back from her hair.

"What news did the abbot share with you?"

He sighed, rolling his big shoulders. "We'll be safe here. Abbot Gerald said Lord Vaughn and his men arrived before us, but they left. If the gods favor us, they'll not realize we're riding behind them."

"How long can we stay? Nest needs at least six days to return from Dinefwr with news."

"We're allowed to stay a fortnight, but the Templar, er, *Yorath*, must keep to himself in the stables, and," he hung his head, mumbling, "the monks will bring food and ale to your room, as well. You're not welcome in the great hall."

Their religion left no room for superstition and the otherworldly magic of Mother Earth, while Eleri lived as her father did—with one foot in each, respecting both Christian and pagan beliefs.

She pinched her lips together, feeling bitter but not surprised. "'Twill be a relief to not endure their stares."

Two days passed with no news, until any diversion became welcome for Eleri. On the night of the second day, she awoke to the sound of male voices speaking in tones so soft they were nearly carried away by the north wind outside her tiny chamber. Verily, the white monks. Once during the time of their stay, she'd left her cell to walk to the courtyard for a few moments of sunshine, but the sight of the brothers' scowls of disapproval had her returning to her room, furious and insulted. So she'd tolerated the chilly room with its poorly constructed walls and the cold that seeped in to stir around her bed while she tried and failed miserably to sleep without wondering about her captive.

Left alone in the stables, would Warren be able to keep his promise to not utter a word? Or would he break like a coward and beg the abbot's help to return him to his people?

Sayer, being the good friend he was, had visited each day, but each night he chugged down the abbey's ale and then slept next door like a log. He wouldn't be awake at this late hour, nor would he hear the murmurs of the soft-spoken monks.

She pulled her wool cover from the bed and wrapped it around her shoulders to go and see what the commotion was about.

Upon her approach, a pair of priests seated on a stone bench ended their conversation, a swirl of Norman words. Wide-eyed, they sprang to their feet.

"Forgive us, Princess. We didn't mean to wake you," the taller monk said quickly in her tongue.

"Aye." The other priest's head bobbed, as he stared at the ground. "Our apologies. We were just returning from matins."

She forgave them, and no sooner had the words left her mouth, the pair scattered in opposite directions, leaving her alone in the darkened yard.

Eleri sighed and dropped to the vacant bench. Sadly, even conversing with the dour monks would've been preferable to spending another evening alone. Now the long open walkway was completely empty. She braced her elbows on her knees and propped her chin in her hand. Usually she spent her sleepless hours waiting on the watery spirits to name the dying, but she could not commune with the *cyhyraeth* without the monks knowing.

"What did the priests say to you just now?"

Her stomach flipped, hearing Warren's low, silky voice whispering in the darkness. She turned in his direction, but saw nothing in the shadows. How long had he been standing there watching the priests…or her door? "Nothing. You shouldn't be out here."

"Why? What's wrong with the mute venturing out at night?" He sauntered into the moonlight and sat beside her.

Her side tingled from the warmth of his presence. She pulled her blanket tighter around her shoulders. "Shhh. They might hear. Besides, they're very intimidated by your presence."

"And yours, 'twould seem. I think they would've jumped out of their robes if you'd threatened them." He leaned closer until his arm brushed hers, and gave her a half-smile. "Your herbs are like a plague on my skin. I scrubbed half the afternoon, and the smell is still there. But…they're all abed now. It's just us. Would you like to know what these two were saying before you came outside?"

She felt her face blanch. "Eavesdropping, my lord? Go on, what did they say?"

"Apparently they believe your pagan soul is lost to the devil and that you speak to the dead." His voice held no humor or sarcasm, only contemplation—almost reverence. He took her hand and folded his around it. His warmth spread through her—a most comforting sensation, but he stared distractedly at his knees. "Of course I didn't believe them, but there are those who would appreciate that ability. Myself included. To be able to speak to the departed one last time…"

Regret filled his voice. She squeezed his hand, and his gaze lifted to hers. "'Tis more a curse than a gift."

Astonishingly, he didn't argue against her ability. Instead, he drew her hand to his mouth and warmed her frigid fingers with his breath. "You know, I *do* regret that I didn't learn your language, Eleri."

"Why? Do you feel left out of my conversations with Sayer?"

He looked up, staring at her for a long moment. "Nay. If I'd understood Welsh, I would've known the words the traitor had used when we arrived, misinforming your people that we were there to do you harm." He then bent to her ear and whispered, "Do you think if I were Welsh, you would agree to marry me?"

She smiled, glad to be done talking about the dead. "Nay. My father only gave me to Owain because he was prince of the territory he wished to control. When you meet Father you'll understand. He's a very proud ruler but fair. The Aberffraw family is descended from Rhodri the Great, so I'm expected to marry royalty."

A wolfish grin spread on his face. "Ah. *Tres bien*." He drew her hand to his lips and kissed her palm. "Would it help my offer of an alliance between us if I told you my father was a king?"

Eleri reeled back, tugging her hand free to cradle against her chest. "You jest, Norman, but 'tis no joke. All of my sisters were wed to princes. I was the last to wed, waiting whilst my father searched for the best match. I could've died a maiden."

His eyes searched hers for a long moment, leaving her to wonder at his thoughts. She wished she'd kept her candor to herself. Speaking of matters of the bedchamber with such an experienced man made her hot with embarrassment.

"I wish I were jesting." He sighed after a length. "There were several of us born to different royal mistresses. Mine, Gieva de Tracy, bore Henry two children, including myself. My father acknowledged my little sister's birthright, but died before acknowledging me. Though after everything…I am for certes he never would've claimed me as his son if he'd lived to be a hundred." He shrugged.

There was nothing but honesty in his words and his resigned demeanor.

Her breath rushed out as horror washed over her. "Oh Goddess! I've kidnapped a king's son!"

"A bastard son," he said lightheartedly. "And now another king, my cousin, sits upon my father's throne, so you see I have royal blood, but again naught else to recommend me, except…that which I've fought for."

He leaned back and the shadows hid his face. Eleri longed to see him better, to search his expression at the moment. She recalled his body: the scars, dark skin, muscles and calluses of a knight—aye, he'd fought hard.

"I'm sorry, Warren," she whispered.

Sorry his father had passed away so recently, leaving him without making peace…sorry she'd treated him as a marauding villain, and…

Sorry they'd started as enemies.

She winced as another thought struck her. "So this is why you have assassins trying to kill you?"

"Perhaps." His voice was clipped. "There are some who hate me for other reasons."

Her gut squeezed. She couldn't change her course of action—not when Lew's life hung in the balance—but she couldn't make herself hate Warren, either.

Beyond caring if any priests were watching, she followed her instincts, letting go of her blanket to cup his face in her hands. The rough texture of his skin against her palms felt masculine and earthy. Natural.

His fascinating eyes widened with surprise, then his gaze lowered to her lips as the sadness he'd shared dissolved into the same hunger she felt.

Desire surged within Eleri. Unable to stop herself, she brought her mouth to his.

His hands slid into her hair, holding her as he returned her kiss. She wouldn't have ended it, though. Not when his touch brought such relief to her. His lips brushed over the corners of her mouth, the tip of his tongue slowly following the curve of her lower lip before she opened to him. His fingers caressed the back of her neck, sliding up and down, awakening her senses to the pure pleasure of his coarse skin against hers. She suckled his tongue, and he groaned.

His hands floated down her body before fisting in the front of her thin chemise.

Oh, Goddess! She'd come outside dressed in her sleeping garment.

Panicking, she reached for the blanket, but Warren's fingers captured her breast and fondled her flesh. "We're alone," he murmured.

Her body tingled with wicked pleasure, her fear seeping away into the night.

He lifted his head and kissed her cheek then beneath her ear and along her jaw. He grabbed her waist and urged her closer, angling his head to nibble her neck. As he descended her collarbone and dropped a trail of warm kisses along the edge of her bodice, she arched her back, giving him complete permission.

His hand slid around her thigh and pulled her legs across his lap. Then, with his arms wrapped securely around her, he lowered his mouth to her breast and took her nipple through the fabric of her gown. Heat fanned through her.

She gripped his solid shoulder in one hand and sank her other hand into his hair, holding him to her breast. "Warren—"

He lifted his head, cradling her damp bosom in his hand. His thumb stroked across her hardened nipple, sending darts of delight through her as he regarded her. "Mmm…I like the sound of my name on your lips. I would like it even better if we didn't have to whisper. Come with me." He set her on her feet, rising as he steadied her against his chest.

Her knees wobbled, and she was thankful for his arms around her. He took her hand to lead her toward the stables.

"No." She pulled against him, unwilling to end things, but also not wanting to risk discovery. Mayhap just this once they could act not as enemies, but as equals. Tomorrow would probably find her nursing regrets, but tonight—just this once—she would take what she wanted. "Not the barn. In here."

He glanced over the top of her head at her door and smiled.

Chapter Eight

Warren's heart was pounding like a green youth's by the time he shut the door and Eleri lit a sconce in the wall, illuminating her bedchamber. She held her blanket in front of her chemise as she backed away from him, moving toward the bed. Her eyes were rounded, her lips cherry red from their kisses.

He needed time to calm his racing pulse and allow her to do the same if he was going to make love to her without acting like some berserker gone too long at sea. She deserved better.

She was a princess, so she needed the gentle hands of a prince.

He scanned the room. There were no other furnishings, only the bed, narrow yet serviceable for their purposes, covered in furs and blankets befitting a royal visitor of the abbey. The walls, however, needed patching. The firelight danced from the night breeze leaking through.

No wonder her fingers were so cold.

He frowned as an angry vein kicked in his neck.

"The room is not to your liking, my lord?"

His gaze swept back to her. Still clinging to her blanket, she regarded him with a regal tilt of her chin.

He smiled. "Better than sleeping on the ground and in the trees. I'll warrant 'tis not the accommodations either of us prefers, but we'll make the most of it, *oui*?"

She nodded with a faint smile.

So beautiful. He pushed his hair from his forehead to keep from reaching for her.

Why was this so difficult?

If he waited too long she might change her mind. At any moment she might recall the evils his countrymen had caused her people and send him away with a boot to the backside. There was no time to waste if he wanted to woo her.

Pouncing on her isn't the answer either.

He cleared his throat, though he was far from parched—fairly salivating, actually, for another taste of Eleri. "Did, um…the brothers leave you aught to drink?"

"Aye." She went to a tray left in the corner of the room and retrieved a cup, which she filled and brought back.

He took the vessel and his unsteady fingers brushed hers in the exchange.

Eleri looked away, causing the single plait of her hair to fall over her shoulder.

He tossed back the mead, barely allowing the sweet taste of honey to linger on his tongue. He had other cravings to satisfy.

"Delicious. *Merci.*" He returned the empty cup to her. She replaced the vessel in the corner, and he found his words. "I liked your hair down, the way it was when we arrived here. Would you—"

Her fingers unwound the braid before he could finish his request. There was something artless in her movements, a lack of confidence—the only uncertainty he'd witnessed from her—and it pulled at him like a siren's song.

His feet led him closer until he stood less than an arm's length away from her. He reached tentatively for her hair, finishing the work for her. His fingers slid through the unraveled, silken waves, and he held them in the firelight, watching the shimmering color that rivaled the flame.

Red gold against silver skin. Everything about her radiated like the moon and the sun. A treasure to plunder.

Only this treasure would hopefully soon belong to him. A prize that none could match or better—not even his royal kin.

Excitement fueled his ardor. He unfastened his belt, and it fell to the floor along with his sword, making a loud twang. Eleri jumped, and he cursed himself beneath his breath for being a fool again.

"Forgive me for my eagerness. Since I set eyes on you, I've wanted this moment." He took her by the shoulders and caressed the elegant curve of her arm muscles beneath his thumbs. An archer, she had the limbs of Diana, he reminded himself, sending more blood to his already painful member.

Her tongue darted out to wet her lips, and he was nearly lost. "I should be honest, my lord. I may be a widow, but I'm not very familiar… that is to say, I'm not as practiced as you might—"

"Shhh." He put a finger to her mouth when her gaze avoided his. He smiled. "I suspect I'll enjoy creating new experiences with you. Let's leave the past outside your door. In here, there's only you and me, *n'est-ce pas*?"

She nodded, lifting her chin a notch higher as she met his gaze. His chest tightened with respect.

Mayhap Stephen had thought he'd been playing a terrible trick on his cousin and rival for the throne by sending him here to claim his so-called willing bride, but in fact, there was surely no other woman who could arouse Warren with such fervor as the fiery shield maiden.

"Put down your blanket, Eleri, and remove your clothing," he said, his voice gone hoarse. "I want to see you."

After another nod, she tossed the blanket on the bed. Her hands made fists in the sides of her gown, then she pulled it over her head to drop on the ground between them.

Her flesh was pure alabaster with the exception of her chest, which was a rosy shade of pink beneath his scrutiny. Her breasts were as perfect as he'd imagined when he'd explored them with his hands earlier. Heavy yet pert. The nipples stood in hardened buds, ripe berries he wished to lick and suckle. Every inch of her was extraordinary.

With light fingertips, he traced the sway of her narrow waist down the feminine curve of her hip—smooth, supple skin that converged in a triangle at the juncture of her thighs where a small vee of gilt-red curls brought life to his fantasies.

How could he put into words how much he appreciated her beauty when his brain had relocated to his groin? He managed to murmur, "*Ma cœur.*"

Her hip cocked, and she crossed her arms beneath her breasts, which pushed them closer beneath his view. "Should you not disrobe as well, milord?"

Eleri scowled at herself, hurrying to the sanctuary of the bed while Warren removed his tunic. He probably didn't like what he saw, the same as Owain hadn't.

Merlin's beard! You said you wouldn't think of anyone else!

She really must keep her word and think only about the two of them.

Diving under the blankets, she quickly covered her nakedness in case her looks disappointed him. Yet when Warren removed his boots and slid his trousers off, revealing long, chiseled legs and his thick staff, she immediately forgot everyone *except* Warren.

Her throat tightened as he drew near, his imposing, naked form looming before her. Broad shouldered, narrow hipped and carved into hard angles with corded muscles, he made her pine for more of his kisses and tender caresses that always seemed to put her at ease. In his arms she'd finally found the enjoyment and passion she'd been missing.

Reaching her, Warren knelt and offered her his open hand. She clutched the blanket to her breasts and lightly put her fingertips against his callused palm. Locked in his smoldering stare, she watched as he lifted her knuckles to his lips and pressed a kiss against them.

"Your Highness, your beauty is beyond compare."

Eleri rolled her eyes while flushing to her roots. "Must you tease me? I trow well enough that I look nothing like your women from England or Normandy."

His eyes crinkled at the corners as he rubbed his cheek against the back of her hand. "'Tis my good fortune you do not. You are unique, rare and utterly irresistible. But what about me, *ma belle fée rouge?* Would you say I look nothing like your countrymen either?" Still holding her hand, he spread his arms wide for her scrutiny.

Eleri laughed, barely catching her blanket as it dipped in the movement. "You know you do, thanks to me! At least for now."

A line appeared between his brows. "You prefer me this way? Mayhap my form isn't to your liking."

She tugged teasingly on his hand when he looked down, and bit her lip to keep from smiling too broadly. "You just want to be told you're handsome. I'll wager you made a very bad monk, my lord."

"You think I'm handsome?" His eyes darkened.

The chill in the chamber had become a distant memory because suddenly the covers felt too warm.

His gaze lowered to her breasts, scalding her with the intensity of his stare. "At this moment, I'm exceedingly glad I'm no longer a monk."

She saw his intentions when his smoky eyes lifted to her lips, and she leaned forward, meeting him halfway. Her arms went around his neck as he settled beside her. His kiss was urgent, and restraint hummed in the skin beneath her fingertips like a plucked harp string. Then the kiss deepened as he explored the farthest reaches of her mouth, provocative and inciting. She melted.

He kissed her neck, his hands skimming over her shoulder blades, then gliding to the front to discover the slopes of her breasts. She released the blanket between them, giving him full access. His mouth passed across her chest with kisses and tiny flicks of his tongue, as his fingers scaled the peaks of her nipples. He took her into his mouth and…*oh Goddess!*…stoked her need with soft nibbles.

Her fingers dug into his shoulder muscles, fighting wild urges. At any moment she would surely die.

"Let me hold you. Let me touch you, Eleri." He kissed a trail from her chest to her throat. "I must have you."

A quavering sigh escaped her. "Can I touch you the same as I watched you do?"

He swallowed audibly. "*Oui*, I would like that. But allow me to pleasure you first. I want to enjoy you as long as possible. We have all night, *ma cœur*."

Oh, yes. She wanted the same. All night.

He eased her back on the bed as he moved over her, putting his legs between hers. His arousal touched hers, sending sparks through her, but he placed his hand between their bodies. Kissing her neck, he cupped her mound. She tilted her hips, leaning into his touch.

He moaned against her neck. She felt his finger slip inside to spread the dew against her entrance. She'd never known a man could be caring and unhurried. Hunger twined through her.

She stroked his back and flat stomach, loving the feel of his hard warrior's body against her softer flesh. "Warren, I need—"

"I aim to give it to you…and more." He kissed her ear and nibbled her earlobe.

Her body ached with emptiness and longing.

His hand molded to her buttocks as he lifted her. Her knees drew up around him, and he slid down, kissing the sensitive skin of her inner thighs as he caressed her with growing abandon. Murmuring praise, he dipped his fingers within her heat, pausing for a taste. His dark head moved between her thighs and she gasped, shock rolling through her. But the warmth of his tongue sent her headlong into ecstasy. She pushed up on her elbows, giving herself to the crashing wave of pleasure he'd created.

Her release was frenzied and manic. She shook all over as the moment took her. He rose, watching her response with heat in his eyes.

"Eleri," he rasped and nuzzled her throat. His penis rested heavy on her stomach, making the ache inside her return. "*Je suis désolé.* I was wrong. I…cannot wait." He groaned against her neck.

With a ragged breath, he pushed up and stared into her eyes with fierce anguish. She gulped for a bolstering breath of courage as his powerful body hovered over her, and he entered. His thickness filled her until she tensed around him. She cried out at the sudden pressure, and he echoed with a moan of satisfaction. Their fit was tight, but so very perfect. She whimpered with excitement when he deepened his thrust, burying himself to the hilt within her. Too long she'd hoped to feel like this.

"See what you do to me, *ma cœur!*" His body shook as well as he rocked into her slowly.

Her body grew more pliant around him, adjusting to his size. His rhythm unraveled her from the inside out, making her want and want like she'd never wanted before. She ran her hands down his chest, over her distinctive markings that seemed to brand him as hers alone. "*Warren, yes… Please.*"

Her spirit seemed to soar with his, spiraling together, dizzying, out of control.

The pressure was too much. She would shatter at any moment.

Breathless and perhaps knowing her anguish, he slowed, his gaze meeting hers with hunger and the glitter of some emotion that might be gratification. "Say you'll be mine, Eleri."

"Aye," she whispered. Then through gritted teeth, she pleaded, "*Anything, aye*!"

He deepened his thrust further than she thought possible, yet she arched into him, taking him deeper still. He groaned. Then, moving with more desperation, he clutched her hips, pulled back and thrust again. Her bones felt as if they would pull apart, yet she reached for him, taking each force of his strong body. When he thrust again, she gripped him tight, wanting to attach him to her completely.

She reached her pleasure again.

He moaned her name, hardening from head to foot, then stilled with his eyes closed in ecstasy, his head tilted back. For a moment they lingered, perfectly molded as one being.

His seed pumped deep inside her, filling her with the sweetest warmth before his head fell forward, touching her shoulder gently. He nuzzled her neck, kissing beneath her chin as he withdrew. Then he scooped her into his arms, rolling her over, and took her place on the bed while she rested on his chest. His arms encircled her as his fingers played up and down her arms.

His skin was dewy but pleasant, so she snuggled against him. A sense of comfort warmed her all over. She placed her hand over his heart and closed her eyes, thanking her goddess for guiding her to him, for the healer who saved him, and for Lew for allowing him to live.

When she opened her eyes, she found him staring at her. His gaze was soft and curious. Never had she seen a more beautiful man, and in comparison, she wondered at the other women he'd held. Courtesans, the noble ladies she'd seen in court processions.

How had she, a shield maiden of Gwynedd, compared to them with her lack of experience and unpracticed skills?

Her one time with Owain had been hasty. A few moments of grunts, pain and a terrible sense of loss when he'd rolled off of her before he'd drunkenly sauntered back to his own bedchamber.

Mayhap it was wrong of her to want what she did, but she could not help longing for more of what she'd just experienced with Warren. And unless she was sorely wrong, he'd taken pleasure from her, as well.

And why not?

The hard part would be letting him go at the end of their journey. Giving him up, handing him over to someone else. Her father.

He was a good choice. Whether Warren wanted it or not, he would be cared for there. And live, of course.

Then she would have to return to Owain's people—hers now—to

her rightful place as their princess.

Warren stirred and pressed his lips to her forehead. His sex hardened beneath her.

Even now, sated, she felt herself aching to be filled by him again.

If it was wrong of her to feel such desires for a man, an enemy, she wasn't sure she cared. Shouldn't she do as she pleased? Slake her lust and enjoy her captive, as he quenched his own needs with her.

A few days more. What harm could come from a few days more?

Chapter Nine

Warren held Eleri's hands as he guided her backwards through the open entrance to the stables. After spending the past few nights in secrecy in her bedchamber, he wanted to bring her elsewhere today during daylight, to walk with her by his side. To give her a chance to see what her life would be like if they wedded. Living as equals, they would enjoy the freedom of being together in his Devon home, a quiet, peaceful life on an English farm where they would want for nothing. To secure his king's trust, his family's future, and perhaps even his own happiness, he needed to convince her he was more than a mercenary—in fact, a man who would stand by her side. He wasn't foolish enough to believe her when she'd uttered that she belonged to him in the throes of passion, but he had no reason to doubt her affection, despite the skirmishes they'd had in the beginning.

Unfortunately, this morning she followed his directions about as well as she ever did, which was not at all, and peeked over her shoulder to see where he was taking her.

He squeezed her hands. "Not yet."

She laughed, turning around to face him. Her eyes narrowed with feigned disgust. "I cannot walk backwards anymore! I'm too afraid you'll run me into something."

He released one of her hands and reached around her, to cup her firm behind. "Trust me. I'd never risk hurting your backside."

She gasped, bracing a hand on his shoulder, but she stepped closer and rubbed against his groin before pushing back out of his embrace. "I'm still recovering from your debauchery last night."

He groaned at the double-edged sword of his current arousal combined with revived memories of riding her for hours of mutual satisfaction. "Oh, sweet lady, let's not remind me here or else I'll have you in the hay…"

Her arms went around his neck this time, stopping him. "I never said I would be opposed to that." Her voice was breathy and seductive.

He chuckled. "Don't tempt me. The lay brothers are always afoot in the stables, tending the livestock. Most are Welsh. Apparently they're not as leery of me as the priests are."

She tsked. "Everyone is at mass. Why *did* you bring me here, then?"

Her saucy glare was irresistible. He kissed her, then retreated before he was too spellbound to refrain from stealing more tastes of her. "To show you Timothy."

When her brows rose in question, he turned her around, pointing her in the direction of the lamb's stall where the tiny white animal sat watching.

"Ohh!" Without waiting for an invitation, Eleri vaulted over the stall door to drop on her knees beside the creature. "'Tis just a baby. Hellooo," she crooned, rubbing the little fellow's forehead where a patch of black grew, marring the snowy wool.

Warren leaned against the stall and grinned. "The brothers said he was a runt and brought him here where the other sheep wouldn't pick on him."

She nuzzled her cheek against his head. "He's adorable. You know, my father has a large herd of mountain sheep. I sneaked off to play with them when I was naughty." Her eyes grew serious as she regarded him over the top of Timothy's head. "My father sometimes grants his lands… and titles…to those who fight for him."

His chest constricted. He sighed. "Does he? My cousin does the same…and strips them of those who disobey him."

Her brow furrowed. "Would that be so awful, being disavowed by a king you dislike?"

"Nay, but as I've told you before, my family would share the disgrace. I would never allow them to suffer for my failings again."

Her lips parted to speak, but the sound of the door creaking on its hinges brought Warren's head around. Abbot Gerald stood in the entrance with the daylight at his back.

"Your Highness?" The priest's wary gaze flitted between them. "I thought I heard a man."

Warren touched his sword in a timeworn habit before correcting himself. He made his body relax.

Eleri stood. "Nay, we're alone. Yorath was just showing me one of your animals. Perhaps you heard the lamb. He's rather noisy," she lied smoothly. "You've done wonderful work with the abbey these past two years, Father Abbot."

"Thank you," he murmured, eyeing Warren. He glided closer. "We've had many contributions from Lord Bramber when he visits his keep in Buellt, not far from here. Do you know William de Braose?"

Warren's pulse quickened. What was the man insinuating? If he recognized him as Norman, why did he not just say it?

"I have no dealings with the thieves." The princess spat over her shoulder, illustrating her distaste. "The *Gorthwr* may be generous to your

Savigniac Order but they do nothing for my people."

The abbot's stare pierced Warren before he turned to offer Eleri a curt bow. "My apologies, Princess. I respect your point of view. And my deepest condolences for Prince Owain. The Welsh praise him highly. I know you grieve for your husband. I, too, have suffered loss this year, though not the great loss of a spouse, but as the subject of a respected ruler and benefactor of our Order—King Henry. These times of the Anarchy are difficult for us all."

Eleri glanced at Warren, a question in her eyes.

The abbot backed toward the exit. "I came to see how you were faring, and now I must be on my way." He smiled faintly. "Let the brothers know if you wish to have lamb roast, and it shall be yours."

Eleri's hands balled in fists, and Warren feared she might launch herself at the priest to defend the baby sheep.

With a nod, the abbot turned and left them.

Warren followed, watching from the door as Abbot Gerald crossed the yard. When he was certain the priest was no longer within hearing range, he turned back into the stables.

Eleri shut the stall door behind her, leaving the lamb swaying on his feet, already pining after her with sorrowful bleats.

Her hand slid into Warren's. "He knew 'twas you he heard."

"Aye." He kissed her forehead. "I'm afraid so."

Her eyes were round with worry. "But surely he doesn't know you're Norman. I mean, how could he?"

Warren grimaced. "Like he said, my father was a fervent supporter, and I bear some resemblance. I'm sure the abbot knows every bastard Henry Beauclerc has acknowledged, as well as some even I don't know."

"Are you in danger?" Her fingers twined with his, making his chest constrict.

"Not the kind you might think. I feel certain he'll send word to De Braose that I'm here."

She frowned. "Why would he expose you? If he knows you're the king's son, would he not wish to aid you?"

"In his thinking, he is aiding me. After all, I'm with two Welsh rebels. But…as I've told you before, I'm disliked by many."

Recognizing more curiosity in her eyes, he winced. There was naught for it. He must tell her. She would learn sooner or later.

He pulled free of her hand. A great weight settled across his shoulders, the same as it always had when he revived his ghosts. "Stephen is on the throne because of me. William Adelin, the true male heir and my half-brother, perished in the wreck of the White Ship, and everyone thinks it should have…nay, *wishes*…it had been me instead."

Eleri crossed her arms over her middle where nausea began to pool. Talk of death again made her sick, but she refused to submit to weakness. Not now when she had so many questions for Warren. "I've heard of the ship's sinking. Wasn't there a reckless captain? And all but two of its passengers were lost at sea? Everyone mourned for the poor young prince—even some of my countrymen. I was a child at the time. When was it? Ten years ago or more?"

"Five and ten." He stared at the ground, seemingly lost in his memories.

"But how could that be any fault of yours? You were a youth yourself, and of all the king's offspring, why would you be at fault?"

"Because I took William's place on another vessel to be with my father. The court was in France. The captain offered the White Ship to my father for our return to England, but we had other arrangements. The prince was to travel with Father, but I, in my envy, wished to have Henry to myself. I encouraged William to sail on the White Ship." He paused, scraping the toe of his boot in the hay. His jaw tightened, then he resumed his story. "The captain had bragged about its speed and assured us they would be able to keep up and even overtake the royal entourage. I'd said to William they would be able to drink, too, without the watchful eye of our father. Being young and rebellious like myself, the prince needed no other encouragement."

"So you and the king sailed first."

"Aye, leaving them to follow. They say after the White Ship went down, William climbed aboard a small vessel and would have lived had he not gone back to try to rescue our half-sister, who was also on board. The drunken, drowning crew swamped his boat, killing them all. I don't know if that account is true or not, but Henry chose to think so. In his mind, William was a valiant hero." He glanced up and twisted his lips into a poor semblance of a smile, though his eyes were dark and distant. "One I could never replace."

His pain and self-loathing thickened the air around them.

She ached at his feelings of guilt. "It's still not your fault, no matter what you might've felt. Even if you had wanted to take your brother's place as heir, his drowning was an accident. You weren't there. You didn't plot to kill him, Warren."

"Did I not?" he ground out, his voice suddenly full of heat. He held her gaze in a grip that reached straight into her chest and twisted her heart. "'Vengeance is mine, thus saith the Lord?' Well, *my* vindictiveness brought about William's death. I would've done anything to steal Father from him. When there is something I want, I want it with all my being. I'm a very possessive man, Eleri. Once jealous or spurned, I do everything in my power to take back what I feel is mine."

A chill ran through her, seeing this angry, dark side of him she'd never encountered before. Even though he seemed adamant, she could not believe him for a moment. He'd been a Templar knight, and she knew his heart was good. Knew it with every fiber of her being.

"Alas, all I managed to do was force my sire further from me forever. Not even my service in the Templars bridged the distance between us. He hated me." He lifted a shoulder, affecting a nonchalance that didn't reach his eyes.

"Being loyal to King Stephen won't mend things with your father." She touched his shoulder lightly, wishing with all her heart she could grant him the moment he'd mentioned before. A chance to speak with his sire one last time.

"For certes. But I cannot throw in with Empress Matilda either. 'Twould be suicide for what's left of my family. So this sorry knight," his tone softened as he combed his fingers tenderly through the side of her hair, "wishes to redeem himself by marrying a princess. But…I suppose now I've given you even more reason to decline my suit."

Though his voice was lighthearted, the shoulder muscle beneath her hand tightened. His gaze bore into hers, and she longed to…

Oh, how could she! Could it be possible she wanted to agree?

Suddenly torn, she took a step back, but she also wished to move closer to him, to hold his face to hers, to kiss him and insist he was every bit the brave, caring man he hoped to be.

But she could not lie to him, nor mislead him to expect what could not happen.

Or could it?

If Gwrach no longer predicted Lew's death…

She stood on her toes and impulsively put her mouth to his. When she drew back, he stared at her, blinking in surprise. "I will consider your offer, Warren. Just give me some time to think."

His brows smoothed and a smile lit his face. "Of course."

The monks were filing into the church for matins when Eleri slipped out of her cell that night. Swathed in her cloak and hood, moving with the stealth of a hunter, she dissolved into each shadow, passing unnoticed until she reached the gate. Finding it unguarded, she opened it and squeezed through, closing it behind her.

The nearest source of flowing water was the spring, which fed the lake a short hike away. Her footsteps were quick with restless hope and anticipation. She breached the distance in no time at all.

Silence, she prayed as she pushed through the tall sedge that bordered the spring. *Please let Gwrach leave me in peace tonight.*

If Lew was safe, she would marry Warren. The Deheubarth would be unhappy, but she was a princess. She could do as she wished, and right now, the only thing that could please her was Warren with his attentiveness, his thoughtful lovemaking and noble heart.

In marriage, her lover would be relieved to know he wouldn't disappoint his king, but best of all, he'd be hers.

Climbing through the parted weeds, she spotted a form beside the moonlit water.

Expecting Gwrach, she sickened. But relief soon swept her as the form rose, turning to face her.

"Warren?"

His stance relaxed, recognizing her voice, but his reply was wary. "I knew you would come."

She went to him but stopped shy of embracing him. His reception was cool. "What's wrong? I thought we were meeting in my room later."

"I wanted to see if it was true. The old woman has been here already. You just missed her. You *were* meeting her, weren't you?" His voice was curious, not angry.

"You saw her? The *cyhyraeth?*" No one ever saw Gwrach. No one in her lifetime, at least.

"If you mean the old woman who's been following us, aye." He put a hand on her shoulder. "Who is she, Eleri? Why do you meet her in secret?" he demanded calmly.

He didn't know. Tears welled in her eyes. To share the burden meant so much…to have someone who might understand…someone whom she could turn to when the awful portents came. But how was it possible? He wasn't of her blood, not Welsh. So few had seen her. And if he didn't know…

"We don't meet. She just…goes wherever I go. What did she say?"

"Damned if I know. She won't respond to me. Just keeps rambling the same words in your language. What's going on, Eleri?" His hands cupped her face and his thumbs brushed her cheeks with aching tenderness.

"She's been following me all my life. Please…what were the words she spoke?" She laid her hands on his chest, her pulse quickening.

"*'Fy ngŵr'* I think is how she said it." His fingertips traced her face, and he bent to kiss her forehead. "What does it mean?"

Eleri put her arms around him and pressed her ear against his heart. "Nothing. She's mad."

Desperately she clung to him and closed her eyes against burning tears she couldn't let him see. She burrowed into the solid, warm comfort of his embrace.

She'd changed Lew's fate and saved his life. Now she would do the same for Warren.

If the old woman cried "*my husband*," they must not wed.

Chapter Ten

Warren found the frater house at the south end of the cloister nearly empty at midnight. Sharing the past several nights with Eleri, he'd learned to avoid the routines of the monks and stable hands. He also knew exactly when Sayer would stumble into his cell with a stomach full of mead. Tonight however, he wanted to reach the man before such time.

He pulled the hood of the stolen layman's cloak lower over his head, hoping no one here would recognize him. A few monks lingered on the far side of the room, but Sayer's bearlike body sat alone at the end of a long table, bowing over his cup as if he would fight anyone who dared interrupt his entertainment. Warren prayed he hadn't waited too long, that Sayer wasn't too far into his cups to listen and reason.

Yesterday, the abbot's visit to the stables had spurred Warren into action, even though he was making progress wooing the princess. However, she hadn't yet announced her intention to wed him, saying she needed time to think. Idleness would be their downfall if the Normans learned he was hiding within the abbey's walls. Still, he hoped he wasn't imagining the powerful connection he and the princess shared. She awaited him each evening, after all, welcoming him to her bed with fervor.

Such fervor indeed.

He couldn't get enough of her.

For a woman who had little experience with men, she learned very quickly. They'd spent the last sennight in each other's arms at nightfall, and every day he yearned to come back to her. His flesh craved her flesh—a hunger he could never seem to fill.

His pride told him he only wanted what he couldn't have. That she was playing coy, and he must find some way to become her equal. In bed they were partners, then in the mornings, he was forced to return to the stables, becoming her servant, until night fell again.

That pride might have a small part in his goal to pursue her hand, but a powerful need kept him in her bed. Worse, he feared his heart now controlled his reins. More than his liege's orders, more than obligatory expectations of a man bedding a woman, more than *anything*...he wished she belonged to him and him alone. She'd all but said the words in their lovemaking.

He must convince her soon, so the abbot himself might perform the ceremony, putting everything right.

He touched Sayer's shoulder, drawing his attention from his drink and earning a snarl as his gaze lifted to Warren's face before recognition smoothed his features. "Templar? What brings you here?"

The big man lifted out of his seat, nostrils flaring with alarm before Warren lifted a calming hand. "The princess is fine," he whispered. "Do not worry. I came to speak with you."

Sayer's expression shifted from worry back to displeasure. "If you're here to ask me not to kill you for creeping into the princess's room at night, save your breath. I trow what goes on betwixt you, and I like it not. But 'tis not my place to take offense. Her highness does as she pleases, same as any lord, and I serve her.

"But"—he scooted his cup aside and leaned forward, grabbing

Warren's arm—"if you harm her in any way, I swear I'll finish what I started the day I found you."

"Duly noted." Warren slid back when Sayer released him, and rested an elbow on the table. "Nay, that isn't why I came. I need to ask you a favor. I fear Abbot Gerald knows my identity, or at least that I'm Norman. If he sends word to de Braose that I am here, we're all in danger."

"I should think you would want to be found." Sayer picked at the dirt beneath his thumbnail.

"To be discovered living in hiding with rebels?" He lifted his brows, surprised. Not that he disagreed with the valiant Welsh ideals, but he'd always been a loyal subject of England. "My fear is that they'll hang us all for treason. Or at the very least, my liege will want Eleri to pay for her part in the deaths of his men."

Sayer grunted. "Nest hasn't returned. You think we should depart without her?"

"I think we should learn what the abbot knows. See if he's alerting the baron."

He nodded. "I'll speak to the monks. I've found a few forthright men amongst them."

Warren clapped a hand on his shoulder. "Thank you, friend." He warmed, pleased to consider them on such good terms, especially after all they'd been through on their journey so far.

Sayer's mouth twisted in a half-smile, as well. Then he frowned. "What about your soldier and Gareth ap Huw? What do you expect your man to do?"

"I've no notion what either of them would gain for my death, but I've been thinking about who the traitor might be. Roger de Granville is the man I knew the least. Young, impetuous. He was the most capable archer among my charges, but no leader. I expect your Gareth would be giving orders."

Sayer curled his hand into a fist. "Gareth has always been faithful to the royalty of Deheubarth. Mayhap he wants revenge for Prince Owain's death. Unless Nest brings better news, I fear for Prince Lew."

"Eleri does too." He rubbed a palm across his weary face. Marriage might be able to save the princess from trouble with the king, but what could be done for her brother-in-law?

"She worries about the boy's grief for his brother. It makes him rash, blind to the ambitions of others, but at least he respects the princess's visions."

"Verily? Do you also believe she communicates with the spirits?"

Sayer's brows went up. "Of course I do. The *cyhyraeth* told her when my mother would pass. And Iolo…as well as many others."

The *cyhyraeth.*

Eleri had uttered the word when he'd mentioned the hag following them. *That* was where her portents came from? Could they be one and the same?

The guard reached for another drink, continuing, "There's powerful magic in the land, and the princess can hear it. She'd never travel far from these waters. Wouldn't risk missing the premonitions. Not that she can change fate, but she tries. God bless her, she tries."

Warren glanced away, soaking in the warrior's words.

Spirits. Death portents. Magic.

There was much more for him to contend with than Eleri's attachment to her husband's people.

With no birthright, Warren possessed nothing more fantastical than the skills of a knight, some land and an inconsequential barony, but at least he knew how to please Eleri in one way. Together they conjured their own form of enchantment.

Eager to do just that, he stood to leave. The day had been long without her.

Sayer remained in the frater for another drink as Warren exited.

He ruminated on their conversation. There must be some way to use Sayer's information to his advantage. Some way to convince Eleri she was better off marrying him.

Until then, he would kiss her, hold her, worship her and hopefully become the man she could not bear to part with.

With the stain of bracken water still clinging to the hem of her clothes, Eleri made her way from the stream's edge to the abbey late that evening. Her body was stiff and tired, her spirit weary. Her prayers had gone unanswered.

Warren was right. Gwrach had visited with another ominous call for the life of some poor woman's husband. If Eleri tried hard enough, she could almost convince herself the victim wasn't Warren. She'd never agreed to marry him, after all. Yet the portent persisted. Could the call be for another man entirely? Or had she not done enough to prevent a future union with him?

All too soon she wouldn't be burdened by this dilemma. The abbot would tire of them and rescind his hospitality. Warren would then be her father's concern, not hers.

Nay, that was a lie. Abandoning Warren to a life of bondage, one he'd sworn to abhor, would be as difficult as ripping the heart from her own breast.

Even now, her steps hastened as she reached her door, anticipating the moment she'd find him waiting inside. Entering the chamber with renewed vigor, she noted the clean scent of the steamy water the monks had left in her washbowl on the bed, along with a dim fire in the iron brazier, its flames nearly extinguished, but no Warren.

Sighing, she crossed toward the bowl as her cold fingers fumbled with untying the lacing in the side of her bliaut. Despite her discomfort, a smile tugged at her lips. Mayhap she could save enough bathwater for her clandestine visitor.

Leaning over the bowl as she let her outer layer of clothing fall to her feet, she felt a pair of warm masculine hands cover hers at her hips.

She jerked upright with shock, then relaxed. *Warren.*

Her breath rushed out with relief, and she allowed herself to sag against him. "You're here." Just being in his embrace made everything right. Heat quickened inside her. "I thought you were late, my lord."

He moved their locked hands over her stomach, pulling her against his hard form, and she breathed in his scent. But it was different tonight somehow. *Horses and leather.*

She wrinkled her nose. "You've been in the stables too long. I'll ask the monks to draw a bath for you." Where was the sweet smell of mint and trees from the poultice that had adorned him for the past weeks?

His breath rushed out against her ear. It smelled hot and sour. Familiar yet hated.

He laughed softly. "Expecting someone else, *Dywysoges*?"

She froze, bile rising in her throat. "Vaughn!"

She twisted in his grip, but his fingers tightened like iron cuffs. She bucked, kicking his shin with her boot, but he held fast. With a hard shove against her back, he doubled her over the bed, and horror filled the pit of her stomach. Her chemise provided little barrier to him, and her weapons were out of reach. Finding her alone without one of her protectors, he could take what he'd always wanted from her.

Instead of raking up her garment however, Vaughn grabbed her head and forced her face into the washbowl. Hot water filled her nose and ears, muffling the sound of his harsh laughter. She fought his hold despite the piercing pain, and wrenched her arm until she thought it might break from its socket.

He would kill her first, then Warren, who would arrive at any moment. She had to break free. Had to…

He yanked her out of the water by her braid.

She gasped, pulling in air through her mouth. Her nasal passages burned. Finding her hands free, she wiped the rivulets of water from her face and twisted around to confront him, her heart still beating a fierce rhythm inside her chest.

"I don't want to fight you, Eleri." His voice was light and mocking. "I knew you'd come to the abbey eventually. I came back for you."

Some women found Lord Vaughn attractive with his dark, deep-set eyes and thick shoulders, but his heart repulsed Eleri, tainting him as the ugliest man of her acquaintance. Even now, his so-called handsome smile and lascivious stare at her breasts nauseated her.

She spat in his face. "You dare try to drown me?"

"Nay, Your Highness. There'd be no fun for me in that." He wiped the moisture from his cheek, no longer smiling. "'Twas not my intention to harm or frighten you. I see you mistook me for someone. A lover?" His hands dropped, releasing her, but he gripped the sword at his side, ready to draw if she moved.

If jealousy made him bold enough to threaten to drown her, what would he do when Warren walked in?

She scanned the room. Just as she'd thought, her weapons were by the door. "It's not what you think."

"Please." He flashed another vile grin. "Don't insult me with lies. My men have surrounded the stables. I know you're hiding the *Gorthwr* there, but I didn't know why until now. Have you no shame that you would dishonor my cousin in this way?"

By the gods! She had to get to Sayer and send him to help Warren. "Me? Have *you* none, Vaughn?" She crossed her arms over her chest, barring his view. "How dare you enter my room uninvited and handle me this way? I'll kill you. If I don't, Sayer will!"

He lifted his palms in surrender. "I only wished to see if you were safe, my lady. Prince Lew told me to find you and be your escort during your journey, to see the prisoner delivered safely into King Gruffydd's care."

"And when I tell Lew what you've done?"

"I could also tell him about your planned rendezvous this evening. Besides, it would just be your word against mine, Princess. As it is, I'm simply here for the prisoner."

Lew! Why don't you have more faith?

She edged toward the door. "To see him dead, you mean. You would murder him."

He shrugged, mirroring her movement to the exit. "Our prince doesn't care either way as long as you're safe. You're his only concern. You know…I had hoped to ask him for your hand."

She snorted. "I'd drown myself first."

He shook his head sadly. "And you would lie with a lowly *Gorthwr*. He's poisoned your mind, turned you against your people. I'm sure that's worth killing him if for nothing else."

"Nay! You cannot kill the captive."

He moved between her and the door, blocking the exit from view with his imposing height. "Why? Because you're lovers?" He sneered.

"Because he's Warren de Tracy, cousin of King Stephen. He's worth more alive than dead."

Vaughn's eyebrows lifted.

She stood taller, finally having something to fight him with. She hadn't wanted to give away Warren's identity, but the admission might save him. "He's the illegitimate son of the late King of England, and killing him would bring more Normans, a counterattack against the Deheubarth and possibly all of Cymru. We cannot…*cannot* let harm come to him."

Vaughn rubbed a thumb against his chin, frowning.

"Call your men off, and I'll say nothing of what's happened here. We wait here only long enough for Nest to return with news from home. We have reason to believe Lew is in danger. Leave us to finish our journey and you go back to the prince."

"What danger?" he murmured absently.

"Gareth ap Huw and a Norman, one of De Tracy's surviving soldiers, have turned against us. And *that* is the real reason why we've taken shelter here. I do not know why Gareth would disobey Lew and our people unless he seeks to further the anarchy by murdering the king's cousin and sending us into war with England."

Vaughn's gaze came back to her, and the corners of his lips curled with appreciation. "Your Highness, I fear I have misjudged you. Actually, in your place, I would've done the same—seduced the enemy, drawn sympathy for our countrymen—and the pawn has played into your hands." He nodded. "Aye, you are right. We can't kill the captive.

Escorting him to Gruffydd is the only way. Though it grieves me, I expect your father will demand that this De Tracy wed you. I know 'tis what he will want."

Her stomach plunged. *The portent!* "Nay. I can't—I *won't* marry him."

"Aye, it's revolting, but you have already spread your legs for him. He's violated you, and now you must receive recompense. His seed might've already taken root."

He spoke the truth. Her father, if he knew she and Warren were lovers, would demand their union, foreigner or not. Her mother's passing had broken his heart, but he'd married her when she was carrying their first child. He always insisted his warriors marry their mates, be faithful, thus ensuring the future of the Gwynedd people.

"There must be something else." Her mind raced, searching for something—anything—to save Warren from certain death. "Let's free him, Vaughn! He won't retaliate against us. I swear it! We ambushed his men mistakenly. His conroi had come in peace, but he was betrayed by one of his own men. He doesn't hold a grudge against the Deheubarth."

"He might not, Eleri, but the Usurper would. If anything happened to the king's cousin once we set him free, such as this would-be assassin..." Vaughn shuffled his feet, thinking. "Well, 'twould be better if we'd killed him, after all."

Eleri touched her damp, plaited hair resting on her shoulder. She'd only braided it so that Warren's hands would unwind it that evening, his gentle fingers gliding through the ends, fondling her breasts beneath it until she ached for the relief he alone could give. Then, like always, he would murmur in her ear how much she pleased him, how he enjoyed talking to her, touching her and pleasuring her endlessly.

In her heart, he had been more husband to her than Owain had been.

There was only one thing to do.

Forcing back tears, she placed a hand on Vaughn's arm and held his gaze. "I know another way."

In the Holy Land, Warren had grown accustomed to defending his ground against adversaries on dark nights in unfamiliar places. His ears detected the softest sound of feet in sand outside the camps he'd guarded. So naturally, he noticed the light-footed stranger following him through the darkened abbey courtyard within moments of leaving the stables.

Make that *three* strangers. The first two had also waited outside his dwelling, one at each corner of the building, when he emerged for his nightly rendezvous with the princess.

Abbot Bernard of Clairvaux, a supporter of the Templars, had once taught him that a knight of the Order should be truly fearless, secure on every side, doubly armed, for his soul is protected by the armor of faith, his body by steel. Warren had long embraced the words of his mentor and never cowered in battle, but he couldn't let his confidence cause him to continue on this path, leading an enemy to Eleri's door.

Rather than taking the stone walkway, which led to the princess' wing, he veered right, leading his stalkers into the cemetery. He gripped his sword, regretting he no longer had his shield, as he wound around a small tombstone. Three taller stones presented better protection. Ducking behind one, he drew his weapon and wheeled around to challenge the stalker on his heels.

The hooded figure loomed over the graveyard, casting a mammoth shadow over the stones in the moonlight. Warren made a warning arc with his steel. Size was no match against a weapon in the hands of a trained soldier, especially now that his muscles were mended. He didn't wish to kill anyone…at least not before he knew the identity of his attacker.

"Show yourselves. I'd like to see the light fade from your eyes when I strike you down," he called to the trio.

The other figures emerged, cloaks swaying, concealing them so they blended in with the surrounding statuary. None had weapons drawn.

He flushed with anger and shame.

The biggest man pushed back his hood. "And desecrate a graveyard? There's still too much monk in you for that."

The tension left Warren's back as he recognized Sayer's raspy whisper. He lowered his blade. "You're courting the devil sneaking up on me."

Sayer moved closer. "Come, Templar. There's no time to waste."

At the warning tone of the guard, Warren's gaze flicked to the other two, a white-shrouded monk and a hooded layman.

Alarm filled him, and his pulse quickened. "Where is Eleri?"

Sayer made a calming motion with his hand. "You'll see her at the gate. We must be silent as the dead and get you away from here immediately. Lord Vaughn and his men have returned." He gestured in the direction of the exit.

Warren sheathed his weapon. He glanced again at Sayer's companions. These must be the forthright men the guard had spoken of, and now they were aiding him to escape the abbey.

Verily, God must be watching over him at last.

Without waiting to be told, Warren returned to the stables and opened the stalls where their horses were kept. Wordlessly, the group took the coursers out and crossed the open field to the gate.

The monk pushed the heavy wooden door ajar as Warren and Sayer mounted.

He scanned the vacant yard and the small stone gatehouse, which appeared to be empty, as well, searching for the princess. He opened his mouth to ask Sayer where she might be, but the guard was already exiting, leaving Warren to follow. He prayed his friend knew what he was doing, leaving the princess out there alone for so long without any protection.

Anticipation strummed in his chest as he rode, expecting to see Eleri outside waiting for him ahead.

Bane shifted nervously. Wary of the horse's instinct for danger, Warren surveyed the open field and road in the moonlight. No Eleri.

"Where are you going?" He caught up with Sayer's mount. "We must wait for the princess!"

The guard said nothing for a moment, then turned his courser sideways in the path, blocking Warren. "We're taking you to De Braose and the Normans."

Warren's jaw tightened as realization and fury sank in. "You would betray me, *mon ami*? And her? Your *dywysoges*? She won't stand for this! Where is she?" He took a deep bracing breath, straightening to his full height in the saddle and bracing for battle.

Sayer's hand rested on his sword. He shook his head sadly. "She is with us."

His stomach sank. She knew? And yet she allowed him to be taken?

He looked left and right. Welsh soldiers on horseback curled around him from the shadows of the outer wall. The leader, Lord Vaughn, he recognized, riding in front to join Sayer. A rebel archer flanked him, his arrow trained on Warren.

Surrounded.

His gaze fell on the abbey gate far behind, already closed against him, where the hooded layman stood watching, pale hands clenched tightly together in the folds of the cloak. A single, long braid hung down from the hood.

Eleri.

Chapter Eleven

Royal Court of Gruffydd ap Cynan, Bangor, Gwynedd, Late Summer 1136 A.D.

Her father had never looked so tired…or so *healthy*.

Eleri watched the newly wedded couple from her seat at the king's table and stole glances when they were preoccupied. New lines creased her father's whiskered cheeks, his eyes sagging with weariness from keeping up with his young wife, but all in all, Gruffydd seemed as fit as a stallion.

Queen Betrys, sharing a seat on his throne at supper, leaned over her husband as she stole a bite of honeyed figs from his fingers. A fresh spitted boar dominated the table on the dais, and its massive body stretched across six place settings.

Remembering the day Warren had saved her from such a beast, Eleri doubted she could swallow a bite.

Instead, she scraped at the peel of a fig with her knife, pretending to have an interest in the feast, but nothing could interest her *less* than celebration. There had been far too much joy in Gwynedd by her reckoning.

For the past seven months, she'd endured torments awaiting her behind every wall of the castle. Kissing couples. Families. Happiness. Reminders of what she wanted for herself, what might've been, and what she'd given up. Her oldest sister Alys was with child, and Tegan, her other sister, had the twins. Their husbands doted on the princesses, which also pleased her father now that Gwynedd was in no short supply of men to lead his planned rebellions against the Norman colonists.

When she'd first arrived in the rugged mountain valley of her father's court along with Nest and Sayer, she'd been surprised at finding her widowed sire married again. Not that she hadn't expected him to replace her mother, gone three years now—he had several concubines, after all—but she recalled Gwrach's warning, "my husband…" She'd immediately feared she'd gotten the portent wrong, that Gruffydd was the one in danger, and she'd betrayed Warren for no reason at all. Guilt, as well as fear for her father's life, had driven her into sickness. She'd spent weeks not eating or sleeping, just crying into her pillow at night and watching every move the king made during the day.

After the first month passed, it became clear that nothing tragic would befall Gruffydd, a hearty Irish-born nobleman, half-Viking, who'd escaped imprisonment by the Normans at least thrice in his lifetime. Apparently surrendering Warren had broken the portent after all, and the wraith hadn't visited her since.

She'd made the right decision. Still, she mourned.

In Gwynedd, she had always found her independence refreshing—the opposite of life with her husband's people. Her opinion was respected, and she attended her father's council meetings as they prepared to send warriors to aid in the southern revolts against the Normans. She often spoke her mind, and as free as any man, she could enjoy the beautiful Snowdonia wilderness surrounding their stronghold any time she wished.

Still, her freedom came at the price of her happiness. She could only pray Warren had found both wherever he was.

"My King," Lord Vaughn approached the dais, taking a knee in the bone-strewn rushes below the table, "a few days ago you offered me the use of your wolfhounds for a hunt. May I use them on the morrow? One of my men has spotted a particularly large stag in the woods near the castle."

Eleri turned her gaze away from him as resentment filled in her gut. *Wretched ass!* He would deplete the forest of all the deer if he had a chance.

"Aye, ye may." Her father spoke in his Dublin brogue, "I'll join ye. I've not hunted in months."

She compressed her lips to keep from arguing. Hopefully her father would prevent Vaughn from killing too many of his lovely deer.

You hate Vaughn most of all because he reminds you of what you did.

Oh, 'twas true. She'd traded Warren's smiles, kisses, and his arms around her at night for months of Vaughn's disgusting leers. She owed the revolting man a favor for allowing her lover to survive, and he would not let her forget it. Once, not long after they'd arrived in Gwynedd, he'd cornered her in the dovecote and stolen a squeeze of her breast. More recently, he'd snatched her aside in the kitchen where he'd pressed his horrible mouth against hers before she'd clawed her way free of him.

Would she be as lucky the next time?

At least Warren lived and would come to no harm. He was better off with his kind, she'd convinced herself, than with her, hiding from enemies like Gareth. According to Sayer, whom she'd sent to seek information from De Braose's servants, Warren had been interrogated and eventually left with the Normans, presumably returning to his cousin's court in England.

"What about you, my dear?" The king leaned around Betrys to look at her. "Ye've not been hunting since ye've been home. You used to keep my table laden with venison."

Her sire's brows knit with concern. He knew nothing about Warren or the sadness overwhelming her. If she refused to participate in her favorite sport he would recognize something was wrong. Vaughn would tell him that she and Warren had been lovers, and her father would be livid. His history with the Normans was long and complicated, his hatred deep. She loved her father too much to disappoint him, especially when he was so happy.

She pasted on a smile. "Aye. Of course I'll join your hunt. I'll bring Nest, too."

The next morrow, she was saddened to find that hunting the Menai woods offered her no pleasure, either. She and her servant rode across the moorland with the courtiers, as she had dozens of times before. Out of habit, she stuck out her tongue to taste the tang of the nearby Irish Sea filling the air, but the familiar salty flavor yielded no satisfaction.

Ruefully, she shifted her bow and quiver on her back, preparing herself for the long day ahead.

How had she come to such a dismal place in her life that she preferred the solitude of her bedchamber to the beauty of Mother Goddess's woods?

She felt Nest's eyes upon her as they followed the horses and wolfhounds into a grove of oaks.

"If you'd like to go back, I'll make your excuses, Your Highness."

The men fanned out to flush the stags.

Even when she felt like hunting, she preferred to stalk her prey in a way that gave the deer more chance to escape.

Eleri shook her head. "Thank you, Nest, but I'll be fine."

Her friend glanced away, but she caught the scowl of disapproval on her face. The day after they'd returned Warren to the Normans, Nest had arrived with news from Deheubarth. Lew was fine and had no idea why Gareth had suddenly quit him to conspire with an enemy. In fact, Lew's attacks against the Normans had been so effective that he'd been offered a truce from the English king. When Nest had left Castell Dinefwr, the prince had been awaiting an envoy carrying terms of agreement from England.

Nest's good news brought little comfort to Eleri. She'd broken into tears and was forced to admit the reason why. The entente came too late—if only Deheubarth's council had reconciled before she'd betrayed Warren he might've been safe from Gwrach's prediction.

Nest, younger than her, had been unable to console her with words. She'd been mistreated badly at the hands of the invaders, so naturally she despised Normans even more than Eleri once had.

"You're still not eating enough, Eleri." Her dark eyes flashed with censure. "I watched you in the hall last night, picking at your food, and now…you'll be lucky if you can draw your own bow."

"I can!"

"Not from back here, behind these fools. They'll scare all the game away first."

"I trow I'll take the largest animal. I'd love to see the look on Vaughn's face!"

"So would I. Now you sound more like *my dywysoges*." Nest grinned, and Eleri felt her heart lighten a bit, witnessing such a rarity.

Leaving her friend, she urged her horse over the thicket, charging west of the others. The woods grew closer, the forest more dense. No wolfhounds could manage the thorny scrub where she was headed, which made it ideal for fleeing deer.

As she guided her mount over fallen trees, sailing high above the guelder rose with its branches full of ripe berries, she made her form small against the horse. Listening to the forest, she ignored the sounds of the winded animal and the far-away hunters. This was how alert she should've been when she'd come upon the wounded boar. Pushing Warren firmly out of her thoughts, she became part of the woods.

Out of the corner of her eye, she saw the flare of a stag's tail. Her heart took flight, and she set chase. The gorgeous red deer bounded over obstacle after obstacle. She chastised herself inwardly; if she'd been less melancholy and obstinate, she would've taken a few of the hounds for herself and cornered the animal easily. As it was, she could only aim her arrows and hope for the best.

Guiding her horse with her legs, she selected an arrow from her quiver, pulled back the string and froze—

A pure white hart wandered into the clearing ahead, oblivious to the first stag disappearing deeper into the woods. It turned its massive antlered head, capturing Eleri in its stare.

The ethereal moment seemed to suspend time. She pulled up, stilling her mount as her breath caught in awe and admiration. The beast could've been made of marble, pristine. Glaring at her as if seeing into her soul, the hart lifted his snout, and promptly sniffed with disdain. Then as suddenly as it had appeared, it lumbered on its way.

What was the story her mother had once told her? A white stag meant something…

Oh, aye! In the Mabinogion tale when Pwyll trespassed on Arawn's hunting grounds, the white deer symbolized stepping beyond one's bounds.

But she had never done so. Had she not always followed the portents, carrying out the actions Mother Goddess chose for her? Well…all but for sparing Lew and then later, Warren.

Their passionate nights had been a taboo worth breaking.

"You should've made the shot," Vaughn called, riding up beside her.

Eleri wheeled around to face him, notching her arrow reflexively.

He made a half-smile, but his gaze followed her weapon. "Not at me. The stag. Such a trophy, especially for a woman."

Eleri relaxed, letting her weapon rest in her lap. At least with Nest nearby, she had only to shout for help. She shouldn't have to fend off his groping hands.

"He's not for killing, my lord. Too rare. You wouldn't risk it, either."

"Ah, the legend. Right." He rolled his shoulders, looking more confident now that she'd put her bow down. "And you would never do anything that contradicts the Ancients, would you? I can't say as I'd blame you. The elders in Deheubarth are probably quaking with worry now that you're away. You're their closest link to the Otherworld. How will they know when to make war or when disease is amongst them? Lew is pissing himself by now."

He edged closer, leaning over to snatch the strap of her quiver in his gloved hand. Her horse, sensing the shifting of her weight, sidestepped in Vaughn's direction as he tugged her toward him, and the tightening of the leather against her shoulder brought her far too close to his repugnant, smiling face.

"Let go, Vaughn." She pulled against his grasp, but failed to free herself.

"Eleri, marry me. Together we'll rule Deheubarth and one day all of Cymru." His leg brushed hers as their jittery horses tried to move apart. Undeterred, he angled his mouth toward hers. The tight space rendered her bow useless, so she dropped the arrow, palming the dagger on her hip instead and bringing it to bear on his neck.

Beneath her blade, Vaughn's throat moved, but he continued to leer. "Come now, Princess. You know Lew is an ineffective ruler. He had not the ballocks to lead our ambush of the Norman conroi. The Council barely listens to him. But the two of us"—his gaze crawled over her breasts and stomach—"would make the child who would become High King."

Her stomach twisted with disgust at the thought of his touch. "You think far too highly of your—"

"*Dywysoges*!" Nest called, her courser bounding over the brush. "The hunt is over. Your father is calling a council meeting." Her eyes narrowed as she took in Vaughn's hold on her mistress.

He released Eleri and backed away.

She took a small breath, sending up a quick prayer of thanks for her fierce friend. "Right now?"

"Aye," Nest panted, presumably from hurrying to catch up with her. She ignored Vaughn as she moved closer. "Sayer is back with news of a new revolt in the south. You've been asked to attend the council, Your Highness."

Shortly after the party returned to the castell, the atmosphere of the Council hall was rife with nervous expectation. Seated at the table in her father's court, Eleri nodded at Sayer in greeting as he entered the hall. He'd been gone three sennights or more, the longest she'd ever been parted from her guardian in her life. He looked haggard, his eyes red and skin burnished from riding the open moorland in full summer sunshine.

Her father's marshal made introductions. Then, looking tense and uncomfortable, Sayer returned greetings from the esteemed elders seated around the table, which included the lords of Anglesey, Gwynedd and the prince of the neighboring Powys—some of who were still dressed in hunting garb, like Lord Vaughn and herself.

"Ye have news of our men in Gower and Cardigan. Tell the rest of us how our rebels have fared against the Norman strongholds." Her father rested against the arm of his chair, his brow stern, but otherwise he appeared unruffled.

At least she didn't have to worry about Warren's safety in the rebellion. Even if he was at his king's mercy in stocks, 'twould be better than standing in the way of her father's archers.

"Well, my lords," his gaze circled the room, resting briefly on Eleri with an apologetic curve to his mouth, "er, and my princess, I came immediately from Deheubarth once I heard word. Our revolts have been thwarted in both strikes. We've failed to take either camp."

"We sent a vast host to both Norman keeps!" Vaughn growled. "More than enough to storm their defenses."

"They've increased their numbers and have…anticipated all our moves so far." Sayer straightened, lifting his chin a notch.

Her old friend had never uttered his opinions on either of the clans' positions against the Normans, but she detected a trace of relief that the Welsh hadn't been successful in their attempts to regain the stolen land. Still, she'd known Sayer long enough that she could tell when he resented something—usually something she'd said or done in a burst of impulse.

Since when had her faithful servant sided with the enemy?

"And Deheubarth? How go the negotiations between Prince Lew and England?" Her sire's gaze flicked to hers briefly as he spoke her brother-in-law's name. "Has our revolt had any impact on our friends in the south?"

Sayer shook his head. "They were still awaiting the king's envoy.

Prince Lew sends his assurances that no matter the offer, he will fight with Gwynedd when the time comes. He says you need only say the word, my liege, and he'll offer his best men, as well as himself—truce with King Stephen be damned."

Gruffydd nodded, and she recognized a spark of satisfaction in her father's ancient eyes. "We will send them more men, then. The settlements I made with England years ago dissolved the instant Henry Beauclerc died and that usurper took his throne. 'Tis time for Cymru to return to the rule of the royal Aberffraw."

Vaughn grinned, shifting in his seat with shared excitement.

Feeling queasy, she rubbed her temple. More war meant more losses. Her father had been successful in his dealings with King Henry in his younger days, but he was getting older now. He hadn't left his court in Bangor in years to know how harried his people were or how many Normans now colonized the south, and how peacefully some coexisted with the newcomers, as she'd seen while staying in the abbey.

Nor how intelligent and cunning a good man, like Warren, could be. Pride in him and a sense of great loss conspired to prick her eyes with fresh tears. She blinked them away.

"What requests do the Deheubarth make for this pact with Gwynedd?" One of the lords of Powys asked Sayer.

Her guard glanced at her again with a slight frown on his brow, and a ripple of apprehension ran through her.

"Prince Lew wants independence as much as the rest of us. He sends only his wish that the princess return to his court and her husband's people. He also, *ahem*," he dropped his gaze to the table, lifting one shoulder as if trying to shake an offending fly from his back, "wishes my liege to know both these latest thwarted attacks were met by the same throng of Norman knights, led by the same merciless commander."

The invaders didn't scare her. She would return, of course. She'd expected Lew's summons to come eventually and dreaded it. She no longer felt at home in Deheubarth.

"Aye, we've heard of a new leader." Gruffydd nodded, as did a few of the men in the circle. "Maurice of London, lord of the district—"

"Nay." Sayer lifted his bleak face to stare directly at her. "The name on the lips of the routed men—those who *survived*—was Warren de Tracy."

Nest had been right. She hadn't been eating enough.

Settling into a slow canter behind Lord Vaughn and the other Gwynedd warriors in their riding party, Eleri held one slender hand before her eyes. Her fingers shook, looking more pale than usual.

Swearing under her breath, she wiped the sweat from her brow and exhaled softly, determined not to let Sayer and Nest see her in such a state.

Her gaze took in the familiar forest of Cantref Mawr, the woods that had long been the hiding place of the Deheubarth, providing protection and camouflage for their rebel attacks.

The further south they'd come, the harder her heart beat against her ribs knowing Warren might be in Deheubarth even now. Ignoring the sign of the white stag in the woods and whatever taboo she might be transgressing, she had to find Warren and warn him to leave the district and had to...apologize.

"We shouldn't fall back, my lady." Sayer's courser trotted nervously on her right side.

"She's ill. Leave her be," Nest groused, slowing to match her speed as she took her left side. "We should've waited another fortnight."

She forced warmth into her voice. "Sayer had naught to do with my decision to leave, Nest. 'Twas my idea to come with Vaughn. Not his." Spying a tall clump of blooming mugwort, she reached down from her saddle and took a handful of the herb. Pinching a bite of the heady leaves for a chew to relieve her fatigue, she continued to explain, "I would prefer to reach the prince before Vaughn does. Who knows what that oaf might convince poor Lew to do if no one is there to stop him."

Nest grunted. "We have a while before we reach the castell. Imagine if Lord Vaughn took a fall in the woods." She gestured at the backs of the courtiers riding far ahead of them. "Would anyone mourn him?"

Although Nest's expression was serious, Eleri chuckled as she slipped the extra mugwort into her tunic for later. "Don't put those evil thoughts in my mind."

"Dywysoges!"

Sayer's warning call had her whirling toward him, but too late. Four Norman soldiers emerged from the brush, arrows aimed at Sayer.

Eleri swung left, urging Nest to do the same, but another group of soldiers in mail blocked their exit.

Nest called for help, but a knight rushed her, putting the edge of his sword to her throat. Her friend's hand curled around the knife on her hip.

"Don't, Nest!" Eleri cried frantically. There were too many men against the three of them. She yelled to the offending group, "What do you want?"

One of the soldiers came forward. Mounted on a tall black horse and wearing a tunic emblazoned with three green dragons, he looked at her, then Nest, scanning them from head to toe. Unlike the others, he'd left his mail hood pushed back, exposing wavy dark hair threaded with silver which also seasoned his beard. Nevertheless, he looked youthful despite the gray. His flint-colored eyes flicked back and forth between the women as if making some decision.

Nest brushed her captor's mount aside, riding out to meet this man who was no doubt the commander. "Take what you will. You'll be in the grave before the morrow." Her dagger was out in the blink of an eye, aimed at the leader.

An arrow whizzed over her shoulder, barely missing her.

"Nay!" Eleri cried, launching her courser at the archer. Another soldier cut her off, the movement too quick for her horse to recover from. The beast reared on its hind legs. She couldn't hold on with her thighs. Her muscles were too weak. She grasped for the saddle, but she was too slow. She tumbled backward to the ground, landing sideways, hitting her cheek on a rock.

While the horses moved in a chaotic swirl above her, a soldier dismounted. Grabbing her elbow, he roughly pulled her to stand. Her face throbbed from the blow, but her trembling fingers found only a scratch as she brushed the grit from her cheek.

Still held in the Norman's grasp, she stood her ground as the leader dismounted.

Tall and self-assured, he strode forward. His men parted like the Red Sea before him.

"Bon sang." Stopping, the commander spat on the boots of the soldier who'd caused her to fall. Then turning on Nest, who fought the clutches of two knights, he ground out, "Which of you *women* is the Princess of Deheubarth?"

Eleri caught Nest's movement from the corner of her eye. Her guardian would lie to protect her identity, possibly risking death. Before Nest could say anything, she blurted out, "I am."

The leader stepped closer to Eleri and towered over her. His lips twisted in a grimace as he surveyed her more thoughtfully. Then his black eyes darkened as they fastened on her wounded cheek. "I see. A damned pity, your fall. Well," he sighed, slipping his hand under his tunic as he fished for something, "this is for you then."

He reached out to grip her chin, making Eleri flinch, but his lackey held her in place. "I am Domenic de Tracy," he announced. "My sister and brother send their regards." He let go, and in one quick motion, pulled a hood over her head.

Chapter Twelve

Poisoned.

The word formed in her murky thoughts after she tried to lift her head but found it was too heavy. Images and sounds floated through her mind in obscure forms as if she were trying to see through the morning fog on the River Tywi. Something had laced something she'd drunk, making her sleep.

What did I drink? Wine. Only a sip, along with a tasty bite of bread. *Was I traveling to Castell Dinefwr?*

Nay, she'd not been taken to Lew's stronghold. She wasn't lying on her stiff, straw-filled bed in Owain's royal chamber, too near the kitchen to be comfortable in the summer. The feather mattress beneath her was soft with luxurious fabric, while cool air surrounded her. She could almost return to sleep right now, but something on the edge of her mind teased her.

She turned her head to snuggle into the feather pillow, when her cheek sparked with pain. A flood of memories rushed back: Normans surrounding her, falling from her horse, and a very long ride wearing a hood over her head. Then, her yelling endlessly at the leader who ignored her while he rode ahead.

Domenic, or *Dom* as she recalled Warren calling him, would likely know where his brother was. Mayhap the brother had even brought her to him. Her spirit soared at the idea of seeing Warren again.

Yet if he hadn't come to greet her himself, could he be ill? Or he hated her. His opinion of her suddenly meant the world. A cold sweat sprang to her brow as she pieced together the remaining bits of her recollections.

If Warren had led the defenses against her father's revolt as Sayer's sources reported, Warren was presently an enemy.

And one with a grudge.

Keenly aware of the seriousness of her situation, she struggled to sit upright, but something prevented her. She forced her eyelids open, though the blinding daylight assaulted her senses.

Goddess, her head clanged! She pulled her hands but they were held firmly in place. Twisting her wrists, she felt silken cords, tight yet not painful, rendering her hands useless. Not only poisoned, but trussed up like a pheasant.

She blinked again, focusing on her bonds. Getting free wouldn't be easy.

Belting out a curse at the top of her lungs, she yanked against the knots.

"By the gods. She wakes!" A woman she hadn't noticed before muttered in Welsh from somewhere in the blurry room. Seated by the wall, she jumped up and scurried out the door like a startled brown mouse.

Eleri called out to her, begging for help. When no one answered, she tugged repeatedly at the ropes, making the wooden frame of the bed scrape the floor, but the binding only seemed to get tighter.

She studied her options, or rather, her lack of them. Her legs were free, but she could only flail on the bed like a fish. No one would likely come close enough to let her kick them. Without her hands or her weapons, she had only her wits to protect her. And if she ate more of the tainted food the Normans offered her, she wouldn't even have *them.*

Her stomach rumbled in disagreement. Laced with sleeping draught or not, food sounded wonderful.

She lay regaining her breath from her exertions when the door opened and the mouse returned with a basket. Grim-faced, she moved to the opposite side of the bed away from the door. Her eyes darted over Eleri as if she were as untrustworthy as a snake.

Speaking in perfect English, the woman said, "My lord says you're to eat, get your strength up." She placed the basket on the floor out of Eleri's view.

The idea of taking a directive from her captor—whether he was Warren or his brother or someone else—wedged under her skin like a hateful splinter. "I will not! 'Twill only be something to make me sleep again."

The woman's eyes widened at her Welsh, and she slid back into her native tongue. "I wouldn't know about what you had before you came, but this broth came from this evening's boiling hens. I saw Cook ladle it meself."

Soup sounded heavenly. Eleri sniffed the intoxicating aroma of herbs and chicken, and her gut squeezed with longing. It would be easy to tell if the woman was lying. "You first."

The mouse's eyes narrowed, thinking. Then with a nod, she bent over the basket and reached for its contents.

While the woman was distracted, Eleri pulled the bonds keeping her hands far above her head. Mayhap she could stretch them loose enough to squeeze her hands through. She could almost get her teeth on her right hand's restraints. Almost. The fabric needed to be a tad longer...

Turned away from the door, she didn't notice someone else had entered the chamber until warm tingles spread under her clothing. But unlike when she'd seen the mouse guarding her from the corner while she slept, the sensation of being watched swept her like the tide in a thunderstorm.

Warren.

She rolled on her side to face him.

He stood leaning against the doorway, strong arms crossed over his chest. She hardly recognized him. A commanding figure in all meanings of the word, he wore a deep blue tunic edged in gilt embroidery over a second skin of form-fitting chain mail. His face cold and impassive, he stared past her to the woman holding the bowl up to her mouth.

"Nay. Don't take orders from her, Gwen." His words were stern yet quiet.

"Sorry, milord." The servant lowered the bowl, glancing about as if unsure where to put the broth.

He lifted a brow, continuing to make his point. "If I'd wanted my enemy poisoned, she'd kill you instead."

After everything they'd been through, *now* they were enemies? Her heart sank.

"I see your meaning." Gwen nodded emphatically. "I didn't think you...but of course I see now."

"Leave us. I'll make sure the prisoner understands her place is to take commands, not give them."

The woman curtsied and sidled past him, leaving them alone.

A mixture of anger and relief brought tears to Eleri's eyes. She wanted to rail at him for the way he'd treated her, yet how could she forget the look he gave her that fateful night months ago when he'd realized who she was, disguised as one of the abbey brothers when she'd surrendered him like some common war booty.

"Warren." Her voice cracked.

Pathetic. Be the princess that you are!

Seemingly oblivious, he closed the door and stalked into the room. Avoiding her glance, he dragged Gwen's vacant chair closer to the bed and sat.

She surveyed the changes in him since she'd seen him last. His hair had been trimmed, and he looked healthy with skin more bronze than when she'd left him.

Her relieved breath rushed out. At least that burden was off her shoulders.

His intelligent gaze finally rested on her, but with none of the wonder she'd shown him, leaving her to guess he'd come to visit before she'd awoken. She'd wager her best longbow he had!

"Eleri," he echoed in a cold greeting, leaning forward as he rested an elbow on his knee. His gaze, dark and steady, held hers for a long moment, leaving her desperate for his thoughts and feelings, some sign of his current emotion. He swallowed, but said nothing.

She could've returned his stare for hours through unshed tears and all, but at the moment her arms ached from her struggles. "I demand you untie me."

"And have you attack me? You've proven I can't trust you." His face hardened, gaze cutting into her. "And *that* is why I had my brother put a sleeping draught in your wine. That and...I didn't want you killing anyone in the process of capturing you."

A knot formed in her throat. She forced her voice around it, working to keep her rampant emotions in check. "You know I would never! And you didn't have to ambush me. I would've come to you willingly if you'd asked."

For a moment he was silent, as if mulling over her answer. "I came to you willingly once, and the end result was far from what I had in mind."

He reached for the sheet she must've kicked off her feet in her struggles. Picking it up from the floor, he spread it across her legs. His hand smoothed the wrinkles from the fabric in an idle pass, and her body responded with an immediate jangle.

He leaned over the bed, stroking away the smallest kinks in the fine linen. "Now that I have you, I can finally control the outcome of my mission. I've grown weary of others having dominion over me—my father, my king, you. Now 'tis my turn to seize what I want and please myself. No mercy, save that which I feel is deserved."

Her face flushed at his ministrations as well as the sudden realization someone had not only removed her boots, but also her clothing, exchanging her riding clothes for a thin chemise.

When she glanced at his face again, she found him looking at her with a bemused expression, eyes crinkled slightly at the corners. "Do you remember my promise to you when you first came to my holding chamber at Dinefwr, when I begged you not to return me to the king?"

He meant that he'd threatened the king would soon return to retaliate against the Deheubarth, but her traitorous body quickened at the memory of her own dark fantasies of that day. Of her imagining he would someday come back to ravage her. That imagined threat was more personal, carrying far more potency now that she had intimate knowledge of him and what he was capable of doing to both her body and soul.

She shifted her legs to try to end the fluttering of her insides.

"I had no choice but to turn you in, Warren. 'Twas the best thing I could've done," she rasped. "I did not mistreat you while you were with us, and you know it."

He moved to the edge of her bed, sitting beside her hip. Leaning over her, his mail snagged repeatedly across her gown as he reached for her binding. Her heart sank again as he touched each of her wrists, inspecting her bonds. His fingertips swept over her pulse points. Checking perhaps for chafing…or for signs that the restraints might fail to keep her.

Seemingly satisfied, he planted his hands on either side of her head and gazed into her eyes. The corner of his mouth quirked in wry smile, though his gaze was smoky and serious. "I remember every detail of how you treated me, *ma cœur*," he murmured, leaning closer, "and I shall do… *exactly*…the same for you."

His armor grated as he moved in, his face mere inches from hers so that their breath mingled and she could almost feel him. His unreadable eyes searched hers. Conquered by his glorious proximity, she surrendered herself, closing her eyes for his kiss, and waited. And waited.

He fidgeted against the pillow, pushing his hand beneath it. She opened her eyelids to see him frowning as he looked for something beneath her head. His expression smoothed when he withdrew a long wilted sprig of green and held it between them.

She recognized the mugwort she'd picked before they were ambushed.

"I believe this is yours. Gwen has more of the herb if you need it still." He traced her chin with the feathery stalk, his gaze lingering on her lips, giving her hope he wasn't unaffected by her, either. He trailed the silken leaves between her breasts. For an instant, raw hunger revealed itself in his expression, old longings overruling his cool demeanor. Pausing on what appeared to be the brink of decision, his heavy-lidded eyes lifted to hers. Then catching a glimpse of her wounded cheek, his brows pinched with guilt. "Your scratch is healing. Eleri, I did not mean for any harm to come to you or to your—"

She gasped. "Sayer! Nest!"

Her words managed to squash his warmth.

He set the mugwort on her pillow. "They're fine. They have everything they need. They're angry and fit to kill someone—*me*—but 'twas expected." Leaning back, he gestured an open palm at her surroundings. "Your chamber is far from theirs."

"And where exactly would we be?" She took a deep breath, regaining her righteous anger with the distance he put between them.

"Cardiff Castle. My stronghold for the moment along with its forces borrowed from De Braose, my brother Dom and his men."

"And my father's men? How are they?"

He arched an eyebrow. "You mean your Lord Vaughn."

"He's not *my* anything!" Frustrated, she kicked the bed.

Humor lit his eyes for a moment. "The rest of your traveling party went unmolested. One of the reasons Dom is the king's favorite mercenary is his ability to be discreet."

Goddess. So no one knew what had happened to her and her guards? But someone did, or else Dom wouldn't have known where and when to overtake them. This would require more thought later, but now her mind was too befuddled to concentrate.

Her captor stood, still staring at her.

"Warren, you wanted revenge, now you've had it. You caught me. Let me loose…please." She tugged on the bindings. Fear crept into her chest. Would he actually leave her this way?

"*Mes excuse,* but I do not trust you after you surrendered me so easily."

He was right. She had betrayed him, but he had no idea how much that decision had tortured her. She'd only done it to save his life, not to hurt him. "Wait! You must be careful. We were returning to Deheubarth to meet with Lew. Father wants more strikes against the Norman colonists. He knows your name, that you stand in his way, and he won't stop his revolt after you're dead or even after he's taken a Norman castle, not until Stephen relinquishes power—"

He laughed, incredulous. "You worry about me *now*?" His mail rattled as he rubbed his thumb across his brow. He turned, shook his head, then moved toward the door.

Good heaven, he couldn't leave. "Warren, if you go to defend another fort in Deheubarth, you'll go to your death."

He wheeled around. "Don't worry, Princess. I'm not leaving today. I have to see to the preparations for the wedding party."

Wedding? She squeezed her hands into fists as outrage and something appallingly similar to flattery slammed through her. *That was what this was about?* She gasped, "You had me captured to force me into marriage?"

The light in his eyes faded. "*Non.* You won't have to worry about that either. I'll not trouble you further with the idea of marrying me. You've made your position clear on that account. While I was your captive, Stephen engaged the Deheubarth in peace negotiations of his own. After my failure to wed a Deheubarth princess, my liege made arrangements with your prince to betroth him to my sister Claire."

"Lew? And Claire?"

"A gesture of amity between England and the Deheubarth

principality." His words were clipped and angry.

"But your sister…she's a child!"

"Ten years. Old enough, or so says my king," he muttered, failing to disguise his true feelings on the subject. His brows drew together as he stared back at her, emotions warring behind his serious eyes.

Despite the ambush and his grudge against her, she would abandon every shred of pride she had to wrap her arms around him at that moment and reassure him that everything would be all right. She prayed it would. "Warren, I can't believe Lew would agree. He told my father his allegiance was with Cymru."

He shook his head. "I don't trust the truce either. That's what you're here for. I'm completing what I was sent to do by bringing you back… and hopefully saving Claire, too."

"I want to aid you. But what can I do against your king's decree? How can I possibly help?"

His gaze drifted over her, reminding her of how vulnerable she must look, how exposed in her thin gown, limbs spread for him on the bed. His glittering eyes took in every inch, burning her from the inside out. He smirked. "We'll sort that out soon, *mademoiselle*. All you need remember for now is that you're my captive…my slave…and you'll do as I tell you."

Chapter Thirteen

After a stomach full of Gwen's broth and a cup of beer tinted with mugwort, Eleri awoke from a deep nap, which may or may not have been induced by more of Warren's draught. This time, however, she snapped to her senses.

Oh, she should not have slept! Her eyes were covered again. How many hours had passed? Daylight seeped through the fabric.

Too late, she realized she'd let her guard down and now she felt another presence in the room. How long had they been watching?

She wriggled her nose. The covering on her face was soft and loose. Still, who did Warren think he was, trussing her this way?

"Get this off of me!" she seethed.

"Oh, I intend to," he said softly from the corner of the room. "Eventually."

A thread of suspense tightened within, yet she was surprisingly thrilled he'd been the one waiting on her, rather than Gwen.

He moved soundlessly as he came closer, and she deduced he was no longer wearing his armor. Soon he filled the space on the bed beside her. His hands worked at the knot on her left wrist.

"'Tis about time," she huffed.

Was he tying or untying?

"You think so? I disagree, Your Highness." He stopped abruptly.

Any disappointment she felt evaporated when his breath brushed against her ear as he reclined beside her, and his hand rested comfortably just beneath the curve of her breast. "I rather like admiring you thusly."

She envisioned herself turning into him, putting her mouth to his, convincing him to let her free with a deep, lasting kiss.

Aye, she had one weapon left—her body—if she could persuade him to release her for what they could do together.

"That's unfair of you, my lord, to have such an advantage. I'm unable to admire you." She smiled.

"*Oui*. But this way you have no idea what I'm doing or what I'm about to do to you." His voice curled an octave lower, holding a timbre of threat as well as desire. "When one engages an opponent, one hopes to have at least one advantage."

She swallowed. Heady excitement ran wild through her.

He brushed a lock of hair from her forehead, and she caught a whiff of spice and smoke on his arm. "I don't consider us opponents anymore, Warren."

"But of course we are. I am vassal to King Stephen. You've sided with the rebellion. You used me until you had no more need of me, and now I will do the same." His hand cupped her jaw as his mouth pressed against the side of her neck in a soft kiss.

Aye! Her flesh tingled from the contact.

He whispered, "I could never forget the feel of your skin, like satin against mine. Don't you remember this? Your sigh tells me you do."

Indeed, she'd made the sound, though she'd tried to keep from it. She should not feel the warmth low in her stomach, should not want his hands and lips on her. But oh, how she did!

"Um, yes," she purred. "I remember how you like *my* hands on you.

All over you. To stroke and feel…but I cannot do any of that unless you release me."

He made a half-strangled laugh, then eased a long leg between hers, forcing her thighs apart to make room for his body. His hand took her breast through the gauzy fabric, and she gasped. Moisture rushed inside her. If she did not do something soon, she'd beg him to enter her, and that wouldn't do at all.

"I'll give you a release, *ma cœur.* You know what I really want, what I've brought you here for. " He nibbled her neck gently, making her quivering knees bend as if drawn by a string. She sucked in air through her teeth, fighting against her lust. *Do something!*

"Are you afraid I'll escape? That I'll fight you?" she croaked in as seductive a voice as she could manage.

"*Non,*" he murmured against her ear, making her shiver. "You're the one who's afraid because you fear you want me too much to resist." He carefully avoided her bruise as he kissed her cheek.

Stung to hear her worries repeated, she turned her face away. Her true concern was what their lovemaking would do to her heart.

She felt his jerky movements beside her, and his hands closed over her right wrist, working out the knot, to her surprise. The fabric cord fell away, and she brought her numb limb to her chest. Flexing her fingers, tiny prickles spread under her skin. After he untied her left arm, she reached for her blindfold, but Warren snatched her hand.

"Not so fast."

She licked her lips. She longed to free her eyes, but the incongruity of his authoritative tone and caring actions had her wondering what he was about. The last time he'd kept her from seeing, he'd surprised her with the sight of that darling lamb. She prayed for the return of more of that kindness—some sign he'd forgiven her.

He pulled her hand toward him, and his lips touched the back of her wrist, then the tip of his tongue, following the line of her restraint with velvet heat.

Her heart slammed against her ribs, and it took all she had to keep from sighing with desire again.

He kissed her palm, pressed his cheek against it, then returned it to her chest. "I like a fair fight, too, but when you relinquished me in bonds as a failure to my country, you denied me that. I think it's only fair I do the same."

He moved over her, his arousal heavy and straining against her leg. He took her nipple into his mouth through the fabric, swirling his tongue around the charged bud. Her freed hands sank into his hair as she bucked with want. "Warren, I had to do it," she panted. *Oh, sweet pleasure!* "I had no choice."

He snorted, his hands tightening on her sides. "You're not sorry at all for what you've done. Ah, but did you miss me? I think you did. Let's see how much."

Before she could answer, his mouth claimed her other breast. He tugged her gown up until air splashed over her exposed lower half, making her yearn for him to cover her with his large warm body. Then he cupped her mound, and his fingers slipped over the slick folds. With a husky laugh of satisfaction, his breath rushed out across her as if what he found pleased him greatly. She tilted her hips, giving him further access.

"*Oui*, Eleri. Your beautiful body cannot lie. You're mine."

She grabbed his arms, meaning to push him away, but her rebellious core welcomed the inner stroke of his strong fingers. Round and round, he formed a skillful pattern, building pressure in her center. She ached for relief, clenching reflexively against him. His skin was hot to touch, his muscles like stony ridges. But his hand was gentle as he continued the sweet rhythm.

She bit her lip as her hands moved higher, finding him bare-chested. Beneath her palms lay a warrior's wall of sinew.

She longed to see him. He was impossibly harder than she remembered. Her hands explored him, causing his nipples to pebble. He sucked air through his gritted teeth. Her touch recalled the smooth skin and coarse hair, each curve and angle, though it was like she'd never known him before. Every time was the first time with Warren.

His flat stomach caved slightly just before her fingers met the waist of his breeches, and lower, she discovered the effect her exploration had on him.

He gathered her hands in his and pulled her upright. She reached for him, pining for the return of his touch, but he slid a supporting arm around her shoulders. "Time for my captive to pay her penance."

He kissed her mouth, hard and demanding, taking her by storm, penetrating her defenses. His tongue swept inside her, seeking, then swirled around her—a dance of triumph, both arrogant and seductive. She responded greedily, taking each stroke as she opened for all he had to give. His palm cupped her head, his fingers moving in her hair, kissing her as if she alone could quench his thirst.

After several moments, he broke away, allowing them both time to catch their breaths.

Dizzy with need, her muddled thoughts finally comprehended his words.

She shoved his shoulders with new anger, realizing his attentions weren't out of caring, but an attempt to gain vengeance. He wanted to prove a point. To humiliate her the way she'd humiliated him. "I may be your captive, but I'll never be your slave! I'll not bend to your wishes."

He sighed raggedly. After a moment's pause, he pulled the fabric from her eyes.

She blinked, focusing in the brilliant afternoon light. Sitting before her on the bed, Warren turned away from her, but not before she saw the frustration and longing in his eyes. He sat utterly still, taut as a drawn bow—hers for the taking.

The golden skin of his broad shoulders drew her perusal. Always a guilty pleasure, she allowed herself to appreciate him while he wasn't looking, her gaze roaming over his sculpted chest until she caught the trace of his old arrow wound. It had healed so well, she only found it when she searched for the thin crooked scar.

She then looked lower, making out the red track of a new wound still healing across his side. Her fingers touched the scar.

"A close call. One of your Gwynedd warriors at Kidwelly." His upper lip curled with contempt.

She frowned, suddenly overcome with regret. He'd risked so much.

He rolled off the bed abruptly. His hands slid under his waistline, slipping the garment off. The sight of his glorious, battle-hewn form made her mouth water, and when she tore her eyes off his physique, she found him watching her with rekindled fire. Her lustful gaze offered him all the invitation he needed.

Glorious!

She wriggled backward across the wide mattress, shaky with need as well as apprehension, her anger fading away. He was so agitated, so full of righteous venom, and yet tremendously aroused. No matter his mood or what he said, she did not fear him. Not for a moment. However, when he returned, he moved over her body, looking every bit the intimidating invader she'd been raised to elude. Her back hit the post of the bed frame. His strong arms braced the wall at her sides, blocking her escape. But at the moment she wouldn't leave for any reason. She wanted this more than life—to have him in her arms again!

Passion's heat radiated from his flesh, making her want to join with him, though it reminded her of his burning temper.

"You've always done as you pleased, Princess. I can't change you, nor do I want to. You're strong, a fighter. And I've never wanted another woman as I want you." He took hold of her gown and pulled it over her head. Then his gaze feasted on her nakedness with savage hunger.

She swallowed a whimper as his dark head descended. His tongue swept out across her peaked nipple, and she ran her hands through his lush hair. Aching, she wrapped her legs around him—so ready to join with him again. His fingers returned to dip between her legs, spreading her, probing the moisture, making her writhe against his touch. *Oh, how she'd missed him!*

He lifted his head, staring into her eyes as if searching for something. Voice ragged, he said, "I told you I'm a possessive man, Eleri. I want to keep you, mount you, fill you, but even as I hold you like this…I am still your captive. Have mercy and tell me you'll have me."

Excitement spread through her. "Aye, Warren."

His hands slid under her thighs as he dragged her beneath him, closing the space between their bodies. Then his mouth met hers again. He entered her, and her groan of satisfaction vibrated harmoniously with his in her chest.

His thick cock went deeper as her body accepted him, quaking with the final appeasement of her cravings. Her fingers dug into his muscles as she pulled him into her. Their joining stirred her pulse to a frenzied tempo in her ears as they thrust. Evenly matched, they rocked together, taking and giving, higher and higher. His hand skimmed down her neck, across her chest, kneading her breasts as he kissed her mouth. Their bodies slowed and moved as one, fluid and graceful. He wrapped her in his embrace, cradling her against him as he buried himself inside her.

He arched his back, becoming solid steel atop her as he gazed down at her with eyes full of unabashed need. Consumed with emotion for this man, she felt her insides quicken, yielding her entire spirit to their union until she shattered with a cry. His lips curved with a saucy gleam of victory in his gaze, and he came, groaning his release.

When his seed was spent, he touched his forehead against hers, carefully cupping her face. Her eyes burned with tears from the rising feelings in her heart. Feelings that were new to her. She'd been married to a prince, a respected and powerful leader, but she knew nothing of love before Warren. And that was what this was, no matter what his feelings for her.

He kissed her, the sweetest kiss she'd ever known, smoothing her hair away from her face. "Let me lie with you for a while, *ma cœur.* I don't want to let go of you just yet."

She nodded, fearing her voice would break if she spoke.

Neither of them slept, though they were still enough. She was content listening to the sound of his breathing while he held her close against his side. Her hand rested over his heart, as his fingertips swirled a pattern across her stomach.

Their future together seemed cursed with impossibility—from the portents she'd heard, to his precarious position with his king—but the fact that he didn't seem to hate her eased her troubles.

Gong, gong. A bell rang somewhere outside her chamber window far below the lord's keep.

Warren froze, listening.

There were men's voices, too, but she couldn't distinguish their words.

He exhaled, scowling. "*Bon sang.*" Muttering, he eased up, sliding his arm from underneath her with care.

"What is it?"

"Just a moment." He sauntered to the window with casual grace, and she admired his bare backside through languid eyes. Standing behind the window casing, he braced an arm over his head, staring out. "My brother has returned."

She glanced around their lovemaking nest. At least her prisoner's bonds were forgotten for the moment. Determined to make the most of whatever freedom he offered, she dragged her sheet up around her and joined him to share the view.

"Is that not good?"

When she put her hand on his arm, he glanced down at her. His brow furrowed with worry as his unguarded gaze met hers, then up went the battlements. "It means our guests are here sooner than expected."

"Who?"

Warren's arm wrapped around her waist, drawing her to his side. He pointed out the window. Locked in his protective hold and clutching the sheet modestly over her chest, she peered down from what must've been one of the top stories of the keep. She'd only seen Cardiff Castle, a Norman-occupied fortress, from a distance. Then, it had swarmed with soldiers, knights and elegant ladies. The bailey below looked as busy as a beehive now with a small party of armored men leading their horses to the stables. Among them, Warren's gruff brother bellowed in the ears of the men following him. His dark hair made him easy to identify even from this height. When he turned his head, she noted a dark smudge disfigured his cheek.

"He's bruised. What happened to him? Was there another incursion?"

"Ah, no. 'Twas my… Never mind my brother!" he snapped, making her take a second glance at Domenic and the fresh mark that mirrored the injury she bore from her abduction.

She hid a smile behind her hand.

"Look there." He squeezed her shoulder, clearly agitated as he pointed out a figure across the lawn. A petite raven-haired child fed a pony from her hand. As the soldiers passed by, she huddled closer to the animal, her wide eyes scanning the bailey with trepidation. "There is Prince Lew's future bride."

Her mouth went dry. She turned to see the look in his tense face, and was reminded of how she felt when Owain had left her to fight in the first rebellion—leaving her with his people without asking if she would like to join him—or even without so much as a goodbye. She'd been hurt, later furious.

She touched his chest with deep sympathy. "I know it's no consolation, but my brother-in-law has always treated me with kindness." She would have to try to talk Lew out of the arrangement later, but in the meantime, she wanted to offer Warren some hope to cling to.

His lip curled with censure. "Her bridegroom would've been her choice had the king not wanted this pact with Deheubarth so badly. She'll be no more than a slave now, expected to bear children…as soon as her body is able to make them."

He turned her around to face him. His thumbs kneaded against her skin while his eyes flashed with volatile emotion. "Claire loves to play." He growled, "Do you think she'll be able to play as a child anymore when she becomes his wife?"

Fresh tears stung Eleri's eyes for the little girl whose greatest sin in life was being the late king's illegitimate daughter.

"I saved your life, Warren." She cupped his rough cheek, hoping to keep his attention long enough for him to listen and know she spoke the truth. "The assassins would've killed you when we left the abbey. We might've been able to protect you if Nest had returned soon enough, but then Vaughn arrived. And he wanted—"

"No more, Eleri!" Warren tilted his head back, glaring at her. "I never want to hear his name again. That night is etched in my memory forever." His hands slid from her shoulders to behind her neck, idly stroking her nape, his fingers threading into her hair. She shuddered from the contact, and he took a step closer. She sensed the tremor of indignation running through his muscles, barely restrained. "You watched me, knowing I was looking for you! After I'd told you, begged you for death rather than to be returned—because I knew it would ruin my family—and what did you do? You went to a man you said you hated. You asked for his help, then betrayed me to my fate."

Her heart wrenched for him. "I can't deny it. I did all those things." She looked up at him in challenge. "What are you going to do about it?"

Fire sparked in the irises of his eyes, and he cast a furious grin. "At the moment? Nothing. Wait for your brother-in-law to arrive for the wedding. Mayhap make a trade if he's interested."

He pulled away from her and treaded back into the room, collecting his clothes.

He would hand her over to Lew? Good. It might help his little sister.

Politically, it wasn't a wise compromise for either country. The prince would want Eleri back, of course, if not for their friendship or a sense of duty he owed his brother, for the fact that he depended upon her for her connection to the Otherworld. But she had no real worth in Deheubarth now that Owain was dead. She was naught to them, and they would respect Lew even less for declining such an advantageous match.

Yet Warren had made love to her, made her feel as if her feelings for him were returned—despite everything that she'd done. He'd used those feelings to get the response he wanted, to use her body to satisfy his pride and need for retribution. And all the while he'd been planning to discard her like a piece of livestock. The crushing blow of Warren's plan was that not only was she a captive and a slave in his bed, but she was also, apparently, expendable.

Chapter Fourteen

Warren watched Eleri admiring the elaborate green court dress which Gwen had laced tightly onto her body. Embroidered gold *orfrois* bands of silk decorated its long sleeves as well as the belt slung low across her hips. A matching golden circlet rested on her head.

He'd brought her the latest Norman court fashions, partially out of necessity to introduce her to his people, but mainly out of his desire to make amends. He'd even gifted her with an elegant new dagger in an effort to prove his trust in her. After three days of keeping her confined to his chamber to assuage his wounded ego, she deserved to be treated far better, like the princess she was.

She'd been withdrawn after his announcement he was trading her to the Deheubarth. A taste of her own medicine, he'd originally thought. But his threat probably hurt him worse than it did her. Seeing her sad and angry made him feel like horse dung.

Tonight he would make up for it, escorting her to dinner in the great hall to finally meet his family. When he'd invited her, her expression had brightened like the desert sun. He hadn't the heart to tell her the good news yet that Prince Lew would also be joining them and that her brother-in-law would expect to be allowed to see her.

He wanted to keep her joy for himself alone.

Jealous? *Oui*, he supposed he was. But he liked to be the cause of her happiness. Despite everything that had befallen him since their first meeting, he still wanted no other woman as much as he wanted Eleri. If she would forgive him of his weakness, his possessive nature, he would do anything to keep her affection. Even if it meant letting her go, but on her own terms. Not his.

"Turn," he commanded, leaning forward in his chair. He pretended to make a critical study of her, though watching her groom and dress her body was pure wicked fun.

Gwen moved aside, giving Eleri ample room to follow his orders.

The princess frowned, twining one of her braids around her finger, stroking the soft ribbon threading her hair. "When you said you were going to treat me exactly the same as I treated you, you weren't jesting. I'm surprised you haven't made me sleep in the stables."

Gwen smothered a laugh under her hand, pretending to ignore them as she collected the laundry. They had been tossing banter back and forth for nearly an hour while the maid worked. Half-serious, half-teasing. Completely enamored of each other.

Eleri had to sense he didn't wish to let her go. Although they'd mentioned nothing more about the trade, each of their meetings stirred intense emotions. First, her resentment had caused her to lash out. They'd tussled, ending with her on top of him, each taking their frustration out on the other's clothing as they tore through the layers. Then she'd claimed him physically, joining with him until they'd both collapsed, her fury and passion spent. Following that, they'd made love again and again, saying nothing of what would become of them. Her silence on the subject was slowly eating away at his heart.

She might've already resolved herself to leaving him for good.

He lifted an eyebrow. "I'm trying to make you presentable for my mother and sister. You may remove the trappings tonight after dinner. Or mayhap"—he rubbed his chin as a smile tugged his lips—"I'll remove them for you. In the stables, you say? Sounds intriguing…"

Eleri turned as red as her hair. "My lord!" she gasped, planting her hands on her hips. When she tilted her head back and stuck out her tongue at him, her headpiece slipped off her hair.

He shifted uncomfortably in his seat as more blood surged to his privates. Their games made his erection more painful by the moment. It was times like these, when they were alone, she would grapple with him until they fell upon the bed, chests heaving, mouths clashing and hands tunneling under each other's clothing.

Gwen bent to pick up the circlet, speaking Welsh. "If I may say so, Princess, the young lady will like you regardless of what you wear."

Eleri smiled her thanks when the maid straightened and handed her the ornament. Despite everything Warren had done in retaliation and later regretted, he'd been pleased with the local woman he'd brought into the castle for her.

He grunted, joining the conversation. "Gieva de Tracy is the one I'm truly dressing her for. Wit and humor don't impress my mother as easily as they do my little sister."

Eleri took the ornament from Gwen's hands, then suddenly spun toward him. Her pretty eyes rounded. "You just spoke in Cyrmreig! You understand us?"

His clothing felt too tight. He stood and loosened the lacings of his collar, suddenly craving the ale of the great hall. "*Oui.* Gwen has been teaching me a little."

"My lord is a good pupil."

He groaned inwardly. "Thank you, Gwen." Following the maid out, he caught Eleri's hand and hurried her into the passageway.

His palm felt clammy against her cooler one. Her small fingers laced with his, and together they descended the wooden stairs. With good fortune, mayhap she wouldn't notice his unease or question him further about his studies. But when he glanced down, she was watching him. His insides flipped.

"Warren, what made you decide to learn my language?"

Hope filled her voice, and it wrapped around his heart like a lute string. "Why do you think?"

Her mouth pinched in thought. He longed to kiss those sweet lips, and if he had more time, he would. They'd not made love since early that morning, and as he'd discovered these past three days, even the shortest length of time he was out of his captive's arms was far too long.

"I think…you dislike not knowing what I say to Sayer and Nest."

He smiled. "Of course."

Her eyes narrowed. "Why didn't you tell me? It's no small accomplishment to learn so quickly."

They reached the bottom of the stairs. The voices of the dinner guests rose in a muffled din from the great hall while the glow of the braziers stretched out to their shadowy alcove, not quite disturbing their last moment of privacy. He could wait no longer to tell her what must be said.

Letting her go would kill him. He cursed the day he'd made his ridiculous threat because he'd known it was a lie. Trading Eleri back to the Deheubarth to free Claire from her betrothal? Foolish.

His heart hammered as he grabbed her shoulders and turned her to face him. "Eleri…"

Her eyebrows lifted in question.

"We need to talk," he whispered. He cupped her jaw, passing his thumb along the smooth place where only a small yellow oval remained from her injury. She stepped into him, wrapping her arms around his neck, tilting her face up to him. And he was lost.

Unable to fight his feelings any longer, he crushed his mouth against hers.

They kissed recklessly, hands gripping each other's bodies, breathing raggedly. He drowned in her, adoring the feel of her soft body and her demanding kisses. In bed or out, they made excellent sparring partners. But now when fantasies of dragging her back into the bedchamber for more lovemaking began to tempt him from his duties, he broke away.

Easing back, a new current of vexation and longing washed over him. He struggled to finish, though his lowered voice sounded gruff to his own ears. "I memorized what the wraith said the nights I saw her at the river. It was the first thing I asked of Gwen."

Eleri stilled. Her eyes were luminous, telling him how right he'd been about the importance of the message.

"I may not be your husband, but even if I was, I wouldn't let her prediction stand between us. Isn't being together for a short time better than not being together at all?"

Her eyes pooled with tears. "Gwrach might've meant someone else's husband would die, but…whose? I couldn't let you die. If I married you—"

"Do you care for me, *ma cœur*?" He held her face between his hands, his heart in his throat as he waited for her answer.

"Aye." She stood on tiptoe to press her mouth to his. Her answer nearly knocked him off his feet.

Hope swelled within. "Listen to me," he murmured above her lips.

Resting his forehead against hers, he summoned greater courage than he'd had in the East or even when facing his father's wrath. "Prince Lew is here. I've informed him you are, too. You can leave with him if you wish, or…you can stay with me."

Eleri backed up to read Warren's expression. She'd never offered him the chance of his freedom, but here he was, giving her an opportunity to leave—a man who admittedly was possessive and proud, who fought against his own fierce need for retribution—letting her go because… mayhap he cared for her even more than himself? Loved her even?

His gaze held hers now with piercing interest. She sniffed back tears. Did she care for him? Oh, indeed she did!

Still, the old sense of foreboding gripped her heart. "But Gwrach is never wrong."

He shook his head, frowning. "*Non*, I do not care! If you stay, I'll not let another thing come between us. We belong to each other." He took her hand, kissed it and laid it over his heart. "I pray I've made my feelings known. The only death I fear is the one I feel when we're apart."

She blinked, and a tear rolled down her cheek. "I love you. I won't leave you again."

He pulled her against him and kissed her damp cheek. When he straightened, a smile radiated across his face.

She clung to his shoulders, scarcely trusting to let go of him now that he was hers. "But what about Lew? If you don't trade me for Claire—"

"You know the prince better than I. Will he give up the union willingly, or will we need to ply him with some other bribe?"

She stroked her lips with her thumb, thinking. "Let me speak with him. He usually listens to my advice. I'll ask him not to join Father's revolt." Warren's face was serious, not at all convinced. The solution rested on her shoulders…if he'd have her. She added tentatively, "Neither he, nor my father, will be happy, but if you and I wed…well, how can Father attack Norman strongholds if my husband is Norman? And then King Stephen's original plan for peace will be carried out with our marriage, so there will be no need for a second union."

Warren's face smoothed, and his lips parted. "Is this some Druid trickery of yours? Or 'haps that potion has put you out of your wits? I thought you said you would…wed me?"

"Norman idiot." She smiled. "I said I would, didn't I?"

He laughed, and the sound spilled through the alcove into the timber hall as he picked her up for a tight embrace that left her dizzy with happiness.

They were still catching their breaths as they rounded the wall and entered the expansive great hall. Warren's arm slipped protectively around her waist, sending tingles of happiness through her as they approached the lord's table where the other guests had already been seated.

"Sister!" Lew pushed his chair back and rose briefly in greeting.

"Good evening!" She grinned. "You've grown these past few months." Later she would have to tease him about his new beard, which reminded her of a younger Owain.

At the prince's left, Warren told her, was Lady Gieva, and on his right sat Sayer and Nest. Claire was farther down the dais on the right side of her half-brother Domenic. Warren had likely planned the arrangement to keep his sister apart from her prospective bridegroom. Even the presence of Eleri's royal guardians seemed part of his machinations to keep the peace at the table between the two opposing factions.

After the introductions, Eleri took her seat between the guards. Curiosity drew her eyes to Warren's family. Dom, he'd explained, was the son of a French knight, while Claire was also the late king's. All three had the dark hair of their respective fathers, while Lady Gieva wore her blond hair in twin braids beneath a pale blue filet and veil.

After a distant smile, King Henry's former concubine went back to her meal, clearly uninterested in the gathering. Meanwhile, Claire fidgeted in her seat, surreptitiously slipping bites of food under the table for Warren's mastiff, Caesar. And the final object of her study, Domenic, avoided her gaze. His cheek was healing, though mayhap his pride still stung.

Nest's hand took hers under the table and squeezed.

She returned the gesture with a smile, and whispered, "Are you well? Warren assured me—"

"Ha!" Scowling, she withdrew her hand and picked up her knife. "I am as well as one could expect for someone who has been kept from her princess for nearly a sennight. And all I had was a Norman's word that she was free from harm." She stabbed her meat ruthlessly.

Eleri gestured for her to keep her voice down. "Please don't think too harshly of Warren. He's done nothing that we hadn't done to him. Now that he's had his revenge, I know he means to put everything to rights."

"Aye. Sayer told me as much. The two of them were working together." Nest leaned forward to glare at him and hissed, "Bastards."

Eleri turned to Sayer and gasped. "Is this true? You helped Warren abduct me?"

He lifted his ale glass and chugged back a long drink.

She opened her mouth to confront him further for his part in the charade, but Lew's raised voice caught her ear in a side exchange. The prince's tone was chilly and terse as he addressed Warren, who looked none too pleased with their conversation, either, with his jaw rigid and his arms crossed over his chest.

Oh, dear. She should've been more attentive.

"My sister does not belong to the Crown!" Warren snapped.

"Your sovereign would disagree." Lew leaned on his fists as he pushed himself halfway out of his seat. "Your people have stolen from us for years. Now you wish to renege on our bargain and defy King Stephen?"

"King Henry would never have forced the match."

Lew grunted. "I suppose you would know. Apparently he never forced any match on your mother either, you bastard!"

"Lew!" Eleri shot to her feet along with Warren, whose hand went to his sword handle, and her stomach dipped. "Warren, I asked you to let me speak to him first!"

Though he didn't attempt to answer her, his chest expanded as he visibly struggled with his temper toward his guest.

Her guards stood. If either man pushed the discussion into an altercation, loyalties would be divided.

She swept around Sayer and hooked her arm in Warren's. "Lew, you needn't rush into a betrothal. Warren's king wants peace with Wales, and I—"

A Norman soldier stepped onto the dais, startling her with the interruption. He offered Warren a brief bow before leaning to speak into his ear. She strained to hear the message he'd brought, disturbing their dinner, but she couldn't make out the words.

Warren's arm muscles tensed under her hand.

The soldier moved further down the table, pausing to whisper in Domenic's ear, as well.

"Sayer, Nest." Warren beckoned her guards closer. He eased away from her to speak to them. "Escort the women and the prince to the solar. We're under attack."

"Attack?" Eleri snagged Warren's hand. "By whom?"

He gave her fingers a brief squeeze before releasing her. "Vaughn."

She scanned the hall. Verily, Lord Vaughn and his men were not among the guests.

Dom stood and drew his sword. "The sentries say he's sent volleys of flaming arrows into the palisade. The gate is on fire."

Warren armed himself, as well, leaving her side to follow his brother toward the exit.

Eleri shrugged off Nest's hand and drew her dagger. "My weapons!"

"Aye, *Dywysoges*!" she growled, smiling, and ran for the alcove stairs.

A throng of men, both Norman and Welsh, followed the commanders out the doors, which led to the bailey and the besieged walls. Eleri hurried after them.

"Your Highness!" Sayer overtook her before she reached the door, grabbing her elbow in an iron grip. "You must not put yourself in harm's way."

She tore loose from his fingers. "I'll be fine. I'm as good as any of these men."

"But not without me." He brandished his blade. "Let me at that cowardly whelp Vaughn. I'll split him from throat to balls."

Eleri gave him a quick smile. Yet catching the frightened forms of Warren's mother and sister, who stooped to embrace Caesar's neck as if her life depended on him, she shook her head at her friend. "Nay. Please stay. I need you to keep them safe."

"My lady, I beg you—"

"You must stay!"

He grimaced. Then after a momentary look at the quaking ladies, he reluctantly slumped off to follow her orders.

Eleri flew out the exit and down the steep causeway, her gaze rapidly scanning the darkened field. Smoke hung in a cloudy curtain between the night sky and the bailey below. An empty belfry, used in sieges, stood between her and the gate where the soldiers spread out in a defensive line with loaded crossbows to thwart the attackers. She made out Warren and his brother's backs as they ran toward the fray. Cursing her beautiful dress, she gathered as much of the skirt in her hands as she could and set off to join the men.

"Wait, Eleri!"

She wheeled around. Prince Lew caught up with her a short distance from the doors of the keep. Panting, he held his blade in his grip. The elaborate, royal Deheubarth engraving glimmered on the untarnished steel. "Lew! By the saints, get back inside with Sayer!"

His eyes hardened. "Leave the defense to these doomed bastards. Come with me. I know a way out."

She glanced over her shoulders. "A way out? I'm not fleeing here. There are innocent people down there. Vaughn is mad, attacking us when he knew we were in the midst of a treaty."

"Aye, isn't it brilliant?" Lew's mouth curved.

A shiver ran down her back at the striking sense of familiarity. So like Owain. And yet so…different. Rash. Immature.

He reached for her hand, but she yanked it back. "This is reprehensible. The English will retaliate, and everything will be for naught!"

He extended his palm to her. "Come, Eleri! Deheubarth will take Cardiff Castle, and your father will be very pleased. This is the Anarchy we've all been waiting for. We'll take one of Normandy's most prized strongholds and two of Stephen's commanders will die."

Warren and Dom?

She curled her hand against her pounding heart. "Tell me you did not conspire to kill these people? Lew, I'm going to *wed* Warren de Tracy!"

The corners of his lips drew into a mask of disgust. "After what he put you through? I know you don't want to marry him, and I don't want to wed that whore's daughter, either. If you'd only let him die on Cantref Mawr when he was supposed to, we wouldn't have—"

"Lew!"

The air went still around them. The shouting at the palisade dimmed while she turned his words over in her head. Shock rolled over her, and her dagger arm felt suddenly heavy. He had spared Warren's life at her recommendation, but had he given the original order to slaughter the conroi on purpose? "You *sent* Gareth to kill him! You…you knew he was coming to Deheubarth with no mind to attack us, just to arrange *our* marriage, and you had us ambush him anyway?" In Vaughan's hands, Warren would've surely been murdered. Again as her brother-in-law had intended all along.

His proud grin sickened her far worse than the stench of burning timber. "Of course. I couldn't let his conroi reach our doorstep. The Council might've agreed to the arrangement, and then you would've been at the bastard's mercy. I was trying to save you from a horrible fate."

"I love him, Lew." Her throat burned, making it hard to speak anymore. The smoke combined with threatening tears choked her. "I *want* to marry him. And he'll be a good ally to the Deheubarth if we agree to this truce. You must call off Vaughn and stop the attack."

She glanced back at the wall. Warren wore no armor, and his tunic stood out in the sea of mail. He moved through the archers, shouting orders, dodging arrows, slashing at rebels who managed to breech the wall. Her stomach twisted with fear.

"Listen to you. You've spent too long with our enemy. Have you forgotten Owain so soon? Normans killed my brother!"

Dragging her attention back to Lew, she backed away from him in repulsion. "Nay. 'Tis not true. Owain and the others attacked Cardigan, not the other way around. But even if they had killed my husband in cold blood, 'twasn't Warren's hand that did it. I cannot stand aside and let you murder these innocent people."

"I need you, Eleri. If you marry the Norman, your father will refuse to join our rebellion." Lew stalked her, throwing back his shoulders with indignity. "I forbid you to aid them."

His steel flashed menacingly from his outstretched arm. He would not dare strike his sister-in-law! Yet…his eyes were full of menace, bloodlust and greed.

She glanced between the slowly advancing prince and the wall beyond the abandoned belfry. She could run.

Faking a step to the side, she broke for the open field. Lew flung curses at her back, following, but she kept her gaze on the soldiers. A man sprang forth into the bailey, making a direct line for her and the causeway.

"Catch the princess!" Lew ordered his soldier.

She changed directions, darting left. The old siege belfry made a poor escape route, but it was the only one she had. When it came to climbing, she held the advantage, even though her dress slowed her down.

Reaching the battered tower, she sheathed her dagger and latched onto a foothold just as the first arrow struck the weathered timber.

Chapter Fifteen

Warren removed his sword from the dead man's side after the sickening sound of his last breath and grimaced, wearying of the pointless killing. He descended the ladder leading down from the wall to the inner yard, wanting to survey the battle below. At least De Braose's borrowed recruits had effectively surprised Lew's men, giving Warren a much-needed advantage.

He paused to rub his blurring eyes when a woman's voice called across the smoky field. His chest constricted. *Mon Dieu! Please don't let her be out here.*

He whipped around, scanning the polluted bailey. Of course, Eleri would be fighting with him, but since she wasn't, that must mean—

Another scream drew his attention away from the combatants to a point high in the air. On the side of the timber belfry, Eleri clung to the beams, while Prince Lew followed her several yards below.

What in the name of Christ was she doing?

"Dom," he yelled at his brother, who presently held his booted foot against the throat of an attacker, "take charge of the men."

Without waiting for his brother's response, he ran to the base of the belfry. When he arrived, he gazed up at the soles of the boots above him. Prince Lew, the bastard, was a dizzying three lengths away, creeping sideways across the beams for better footing. Eleri held fast directly above him.

Bon sang! If he were a better archer, he'd aim at the damned youth, but with his poor fortune with arrows, he'd probably strike Eleri instead. So he grappled the boards, working his way skyward. Sweat beaded at his hairline at the thought of the height, and moisture drizzled down his face. Up and up he went, ignoring the sting of perspiration as it met his eyes, keeping his sights on his progress. His muscles bunched as he swung his legs up and over another board, and he concentrated on his inner strength as he strained—on Eleri, the woman he loved more than anything in the world. Higher and higher. He mirrored her movements now as she ascended to the highest level of the tower, picturing the way he'd seen Sayer managing the altitude despite his bulk, as he tried for the same actions.

In two lunging moves, he caught up with the prince, grasping the youth's calf as he hung perilously from a beam with one arm.

"Warren!" Eleri cried. She extended her dagger threateningly down at the lad's face.

Lew grunted, kicking his leg. His expression purpled with rage. "Let go! You'll not have Owain's wife. I'll see you both dead first."

Warren pulled against the young man, using all his brute strength to wrap the whelp's leg around one of the supports. The prince squawked in pain, his ankle twisting. The beam beneath Warren's weight suddenly groaned. With a loud snap the wood broke, splintering in half. Warren let go of his enemy, catching hold of the next beam down and saving himself from a fall to certain death.

Eleri screamed his name again. He looked up to find her struggling with her brother-in-law, who now held her hem in his fist. Unable to take his eyes off his beloved, he clambered up to join them on the top platform, pulling himself up the railing.

The princess flailed with her dagger at the prince, swatting him with the flat of the small blade as tears coursed down her cheeks. "I don't want to hurt you, but I will!"

"I've no doubt of that. You've broken my heart already." Lew staggered to his feet, freeing his weapon to parry against hers. "You're worthless. Owain was like a father to me, a wonderful ruler, and this is how you honor his memory? Whoring with a Norman?"

Warren dropped the bow and quiver and drew his own weapon. The hefty steel gripped comfortably in his hands. "My lady said she doesn't want to fight you. But I do," he growled at the prince's back.

Lew hobbled around, dragging his twisted ankle. "I will accept that challenge." He sneered with a glint in his eyes.

Lew was green and reckless, but Warren couldn't lie to himself—the youth would be well trained to use the fine blade. The boards beneath their feet shivered as his opponent threw himself into the first strike.

Swords clashed, steel singing as it grazed off steel. Lew moved away from Warren's jabs, but after several measured strokes, Warren could read the patterns of his actions. Though he wished he had his shield, he soon had the young prince moving in circles, ducking more than striking, muttering agonized curses from the impact on his ankle.

Movement from the corner of Warren's eye caught his attention. Eleri had picked up his bow and aimed a notched arrow at the prince. She was a pagan princess worthy of legends with her bliaut flowing around her in the smoky breeze while her arms became an extension of the weapon itself, carved of flesh instead of sapling yew.

"Put it down," she ordered, voice low and lethal.

Lew snarled at her, "Some shield maiden! Daughter of the ancient

Aberffraw line? Ha! Think what your father will say when he hears you defended his enemy. I never felt worthy to wear my brother's mantle until now, killing his foe." He turned as he finished, lunging toward Warren.

He struck a heavy blow at Warren, hurling into him, but Warren anticipated the move, blocking the swing and sidling against the barrier. The force twisted the boy's damaged foot, and he fell forward with an oath. Eleri's arrow hit his back squarely between his shoulder blades, the brunt sending him into the rail. The board cracked, breaking and spilling him over the side. He screamed as he fell—a sickening gut-wrenching call for help, answered only by the blessing of a quick death upon impact.

Warren clutched at the splintered end of the loose rail as he lost balance, his stomach tumbling and his body sure to follow. But quick hands seized his tunic as Eleri dragged him against her, and he embraced her as they collapsed in a heap on the platform. Glancing out at the bailey, he found his brother leading the capture of the remaining attackers. With the last enemies imprisoned, everything was under control.

Safe. The woman he loved. His family and friends. Everyone safe.

She buried her face against his neck, her fingers still gripping the fabric of his raiments.

He kissed the crown of her head and pushed the loose tendrils of her hair from her face as he tilted her chin to see her better. "Hush now. Don't cry." He kissed her forehead, her salty eyelids and her full lips. "You saved my life."

But tears filled his eyes too. Happy, relieved tears.

"I can't believe he could be so cruel. I should've known he'd meant to kill you from the first attack. How could I have not known his intentions?" She rubbed a tear away, staring up at him with eyes full of guilt and concern. "Gareth was his man and would never do anything on his own. He's always been loyal to the Prince of Deheubarth."

"*Mon amour*, you were blinded by your feelings for your people, but that's nothing to be ashamed of. You're a leader they can be proud of. You're devoted and brave, fierce and caring." He kissed her lips longer, caressing her face with gentle fingertips. His soul swelled with fierce emotion. "I love you, *ma belle fée rouge*. I will defend you with the last drop of my blood and my last breath."

She reached for him, pushing her hand into his hair at his nape, and brought his mouth to hers for a lasting, life-affirming kiss.

Chapter Sixteen

Eleri tossed breadcrumbs across the pebbled beach. In moments, a trio of birds sailed in to collect the scattered remains of her breakfast. It was the last of the food they'd brought from the abbey, but she and Warren had been too busy making love that morning to finish eating. Besides, there would be plenty to eat when they reached her father's keep…if, she prayed, her sire didn't cast her away first.

She felt Warren's presence close behind her and smiled at the pleasant tingle of awareness that came along with it.

He put his arm around her waist and pointed to the azure Snowdonia Mountains on the horizon. "I think we should climb one of those today."

She laughed and leaned closer to enjoy the woodsy scent of his neck. "Verily? They're quite steep. Has my husband vanquished all his fear of heights?"

He pulled away, sharing his scowl. "I climbed to the top of a tower for you and brought you down on my back. 'Twasn't proof enough of my courage?"

The memory of that tragic day gave her a sense of loss for Lew, though the jab of pain had dulled over the past two fortnights. Her grief was softened by the pleasure of traveling with Warren again, accompanied by her friends and his brother, and now she eagerly anticipated seeing her father for the first time since their arrival in Gwynedd.

And since her betrothal to a Norman.

The breeze ruffled his hair. She turned in his arms and smoothed a stray lock back from his forehead.

He caught her hand and brought it to his lips for a slow kiss. "I'm being serious. We could start with one of the smaller peaks. Of course, we'd avoid the streams."

Try as he might to distract her, he couldn't hide the tightness around his eyes betraying his worry.

She'd promised gladly when he'd asked—no visits to any waterside at night. She hadn't called on Gwrach since before they'd wed. But meeting her family was unavoidable…and something Warren dreaded.

He turned her back around, and his hands swept up her sides until they covered her breasts, fingers dancing over her aroused flesh.

The hard length of him pressed against her backside, and she eagerly brushed against him. His groan sent heady pleasure through her. Soon, very soon, she would make him her captive again. Their new game, with bonds and a hood, had become their favorite, as they loved to play and tease each other's bodies.

She angled her neck, giving his mouth room to explore.

Gwrach had never been wrong. She'd cried "my son," for Lew, who had considered his older brother Owain like a father, and "my husband," for Gareth, who had tried to kill Warren because Lew had threatened his wife. Nest had dispatched Lew's advisor during the fray, relieving Eleri of the burden of deciding his punishment. Her friend had also shared with her Gareth's dying words—his remorse and fears for his family's safety.

As for the white stag, mayhap the taboo she'd crossed had been marrying the son of her father's former enemy. Or for killing Lew.

She didn't regret either.

However, she was certain Warren had been right. Their lives and fate were their own to do whatever they desired. Her husband loved her as an equal—he'd said as much when he'd argued against Owain's treatment of her—and she didn't fear he would abandon her to go fight in a battle. If Mother Goddess granted them fertility, they would raise their children wisely, offering their greatest strengths, patience and love.

She kissed Warren back, returning the ardent strokes of his tongue with her own, while her fingertips traced the rough edge of the familiar scar on his chest—the wound that nearly killed him and yet brought them together.

When the kiss ended, she offered him warmth in her smile. "I'll show you the entire principality, from these shores and forests to the ancient Druid stones on the island of my birth, Ynys Mons, but only *after* you meet Father."

He bit his lip in exaggerated consternation, then gave her shoulder an affectionate squeeze. "*Je suis transparent?* Are you for certes he will not set his army against me? We have brought only a conroi of men, Dom, and your guards. You've said yourself he won't approve of our union. And Lord Vaughn is back in Deheubarth, regrouping his army, no doubt preparing for another revolt." His arms stiffened, drawing her closer in his embrace as he continued to voice his concerns. "I am ready to defend either people, yours or mine, but if our visit begins a skirmish here…"

"My lord." Wrapping her arms around his neck, she gazed up at him and grinned as heat rekindled in his dark eyes. "Father might banish us from his castell or from Gwynedd altogether, but he would never risk harm to his heir." They'd had this discussion before, and would probably have it many times over. They were both fighters, only now they fought on the same side.

His mouth curved with boyish pleasure, melting her insides. He tugged her hips against him and kept her near with his hand over the small of her back. "*Oui*, you've begun another day without your courses." His eyes crinkled with mischief as he lowered his mouth to her neck and murmured, "But before we leave here for Devon, we should keep trying. Just to be certain."

He dropped tiny kisses along her skin until he reached her collarbone. His rigid cock pressed against her stomach, demonstrating his sincerity.

"Mmm…I agree." Delicious quivers ran through her.

Warren had told her before that Claire would enjoy having a niece or nephew, but Eleri looked forward to having time alone with her new sister in order to instruct her on how to use her first bow. Claire's family was grateful she'd been rescued from marriage to Lew, but Eleri wanted the girl to be able to defend herself if she was ever in danger again.

She caressed his strong arms, sliding her hands around his shoulders, loving his size and strength. If they had a babe, it would be a great warrior, who enjoyed training dogs like Warren, and her sire would surely approve—

"Oh Goddess." She pushed halfheartedly against his chest. "You have distracted me again. Let's gather the others and make your introduction to Gruffydd."

Walking into the impressive, lime-washed hall of what had often been one of the kingdom's greatest foreign enemies, Warren's gut fluttered with anxiety for his wife. Eleri and her companions led the way toward the Gwynedd king's throne in the midst of the room where armed guards, allies and a council crowded close to their liege, likely meaning to intimidate them. He touched the hilt of his sword in a timeworn habit, but when his wife glanced back and caught his action with a scowl, he dropped his hand away.

Eleri had seen through his weak attempts to avoid paying respects to her father, but her vision was clouded with a daughterly love for her sire. She wasn't aware of the harsh reality that some children of royalty faced: when the time came for the monarch to choose between country and family, the latter often lost.

He knew the feeling of disappointing a parent with his mere existence, and he longed to protect her from it.

"Eleri, welcome home." The king's eyes narrowed as he took in their group. A finely dressed woman stood at his side, watching the proceedings with a vacuous stare, and Warren could only presume this was the new queen, Betrys, whom the princess had told him about.

At the beckoning wave of Gruffydd's hand, Eleri went alone to sit at her father's knee. Although he was white-headed now, the old man had probably once looked much like his daughter with fiery red locks. Warren prayed he didn't have a matching temper. "Thank you for seeing me, Father. I return with a heart heavy with loss. Your ally, Prince Lew, has been slain…after he betrayed me and tried to kill me during treaty negotiations at Cardiff. Had it not been for Warren de Tracy—"

The king lifted his gaze and found him. "By the saints! You've brought the Norman here? De Tracy was their commander against the Deheubarth forces. How could you forget what happened to Owain? How I've aided your husband's people against the Normans in your honor?" The king summoned his guards with another wave. "This man is not our friend, Eleri. He is the enemy."

"But he saved my life"—Eleri broke off as three of the king's men immediately moved toward Warren.

He pushed past Sayer's outstretched arm and stepped up beside Eleri. "Sire." He bowed his head, then his words rushed out. "I must speak with you about your daughter. Prince Owain was a fool."

"Guards—"

"No, Father!" Eleri clutched Warren's arm. "Listen to what he has to say! Lew and Owain wished to incite rebellion, but Warren's mission was always one of peace—through our union."

Rough hands pushed Eleri aside and grasped Warren's arms. He planted his feet, refusing to budge. "Hear us out, Sire! Owain failed to protect the princess. He left her side. I would never! And he—"

One of the soldiers produced a sword glancing with uncertainty between Warren and his liege.

"Wait," the king commanded. "Let the Norman continue. I want to hear the rest of his opinions of my daughter's match." He leaned against his armrest, rubbing a thoughtful finger across his lips.

Held between Sayer and another man, Warren cast a warning glare around the circle. Let them try to subdue him.

He took a steadying breath before continuing, "I believe Prince Owain's failing was that he didn't appreciate his wife. Your daughter is a fierce, skillful warrior, and any soldier should be proud to have her at their side. *Oui*, I know a husband's duty is to protect his woman, but where better to do that than with her right beside him? She's as good as a man in combat. If she chose, I would take her into battle, keep her close, yet trust her to do what you—her father—have no doubt trained her to do."

He felt Eleri's stare upon him, but he dared not look away from the king, who was now watching him without expression.

"Aye, she is worthy of her ancestors." Gruffydd's gaze cut to his daughter and the first twinkle of appreciation appeared in his eyes. Queen Betrys leaned down, whispering in his ear. Then returning his attention to Warren, he gestured for the guards. "Let him go for now. I would have a word alone with him."

Warren watched apprehensively as Eleri caught his eye, shared a small smile, then slowly left her father's side to wait with the others in the circle. Still unsure of the king's intentions, his fingers itched for his weapon just in case they needed to flee quickly, but he forced his hand to relax.

Once he stood alone by the royal couple, the king murmured, "My queen tells me there are rumors Warren de Tracy is the son of Henry Beauclerc."

"*Oui*. I have been told the same…by my mother." A joke he seldom made, but the fact that Gruffydd voiced that particular question in private made him slightly more comfortable.

Yet the two leaders were once bitter enemies. He prayed he hadn't made a mistake in telling the truth.

Gruffydd's heavy eyebrows lifted with surprise. "But my advisors say ye defended the usurper's strongholds. Are ye a supporter of Stephen's?"

Warren lifted his chin. Again he wondered whether to tell the truth or not. Shame washed over him that he couldn't stand proudly before this throne and defend his oath of fealty. "I have followed Stephen's bidding by fighting his battles, protecting his colonies, and now by wedding a princess of Deheubarth—though I was happy to wed such a wonderful woman. If that obedience makes me a supporter, then so be it. I have done so to protect my family. But my father declared his daughter Matilda as his rightful heir. She is also my family, so if there was any way—"

The king lifted a hand, stopping him. "If Henry Beauclerc's daughter comes back to England, she will have my support. Your father, for all our clashes and struggles, was true to his word when he signed our truce. He earned my respect. Be ye a child of his wedlock or no, Warren de Tracy, ye are his kin. I see his stamp upon your brow and in your convictions."

The king glanced back at Eleri, his gaze pensive. "Other suitors for my daughters have praised their looks, showered them with trinkets, and yet you admire my daughter's fighting abilities. This I also respect. But I have to know…"

Warren tensed, bracing for the worst as the king leaned forward to speak conspiratorially.

The old man's eyes twinkled as he spoke. "If my daughter bears your child, will he be raised Cymreig?"

About the Author

Sandra Jones is the author of historical romances, including the River Rogues series. Living in the Ozarks with her husband of more than twenty-five years, she makes her home on a river where she writes to the sounds of mischievous wildlife and daydreams about adventure. When not writing, she enjoys traveling to places off the beaten path and attends the occasional Renaissance faire. Huzzah!

Sandra loves hearing from her readers. Visit her website to find out more about her books and sign up for her newsletter with its exclusive excerpts and contests, www.SandraJonesRomance.com.

She played right into his hands.

Her Wicked Captain

© 2014 Sandra Jones

Possessing uncanny people-reading skills like her mama, Philadelphia "Dell" Samuels has spent thirteen years in her aunt's rustic Ozarks home, telling fortunes over playing cards and trying to pass as white. But the treacherous Mississippi River childhood her mama had dragged her away from finally catches up to her on a steamboat captained by her old friend Rory Campbell.

Known to his crew as the Devil's Henchman, Rory is a gambler in need of a miracle. Following the cold trail of his boss's wife and bastard daughter, Dell, Rory has only one goal in mind: saving his crew from the boss's cruelty by ruining him. The only one who can defeat the Monster of the Mississippi is the man trained to take his place. Rory's convinced he can lure his boss into a high-stakes game against a rival, and with Dell's people-reading skills, the monster will lose everything.

Under Rory's tutelage and protection, Dell agrees to the tortured captain's plan. Passion and peril quickly bring them together as lovers. But when Rory's plan backfires, the lives of the innocent depend on Dell's ability to read the situation correctly—and hopefully save them all.

Warning: There's not enough moonshine on the Mississippi to keep this fortuneteller from saving The Devil's Henchman, a high-stakes gambler and her childhood friend, from his boss's cruelty. Touches upon issues of child abuse, revenge and redemption.

Enjoy the following excerpt for Her Wicked Captain:

The only thing worse than dying from a gunshot to the stomach was being the one carrying the pistols.

For that reason, Rory Campbell felt a flicker of envy for the man as he dropped. When the smoke cleared, Harold Best's toes were pointed skyward, the open wound above his navel pumped ichor down his side to soak the sand of Bloody Island, while a pair of startled ducks complained overhead. The gambler should've known he was dead before he ever stepped foot on the Mississippi sandbar.

Best's wife screamed the moment he went down. His lawyer, the second, broke his shocked spell and hurried, along with the lady, to the man's side.

The breeze tugging Rory's hair helped to revive him. He glanced down at the embossed case clenched tight in his arms and remembered his role in the grisly affair. "You're the second. You must tend the first!" He'd received those instructions six years ago in his first duel *a l'outrance*, right after Quintus Moreaux smacked his head with the butt of his Colt. Now twenty-seven, Rory's chest felt hollow, his spirit weary, but he knew the procedures. Snapping into action, he went to aid his boss.

Garbed in a black vest and breeches, Moreaux's tall form made a dapper silhouette against the peach sunrise over the river. With the still-smoking gun in his left hand, he rolled down his white shirtsleeve and smiled slightly while the witnesses were preoccupied with the fallen man twenty paces away.

Rory took the gun from Moreaux so he could finish adjusting his clothes. Then after cleaning the weapon, he opened the box and set it in its satin nest.

"Now we see who's really best," Moreaux chuckled. Rory often suspected killing made his boss somewhat drunk and giddy. That was just one reason he hated him.

There were worse reasons. If he had a choice, he would be far from here, but he had none. Too many other lives depended on him.

"You know, you've been my second several times now, Rory." The gambler's cold eyes were on him now. Dark circles testified to the fact the bastard had stayed up late the night before at the card table, as usual—the only things marring his distinguished face. "It's past time you earned a name for yourself. Otherwise my opponents will think you're weak. The next duel, you will take my place and defend my honor."

To remind Moreaux he was the one who cheated at faro would cause him to lash out at someone else—and the thought that a member of the crew would be beaten because of him made Rory shudder with revulsion.

He held his tongue. Carrying the pistols was one thing, but could he kill a man for Quintus Moreaux, Monster of the Mississippi? He'd often thought being Moreaux's protégé and steamboat captain were the lowest levels he could sink to, but he guessed he'd been wrong. When Rory ran out of diversions for his boss, Moreaux turned to diversions of his own making—usually starting with Rory's crew, his roustabouts.

The price was more than Rory was willing to pay.

If you dance with the Devil…

The flat of Moreaux's hand came from nowhere, connecting with his cheek. "Christ! Wake up and fetch my other pistol from that damned corpse."

His smarting blows no longer sent Rory flying as they had when he was a youth. Now standing an inch taller than Moreaux with arms and legs of iron from years working on the docks, Rory took the hit without shame, yet he couldn't stop the hazy curtain falling before his eyes.

In the darkness of his mind, cold dread replaced the morning warmth, and for an instant, he feared he was home on the paddlewheeler again, waiting for the terrors that claimed him in the night. When his vision slowly cleared, fury chased away his momentary bewilderment. Days like these, he could easily imagine killing the source of all the suffering. In one selfish act, he could take one of the pistols, jab it into Moreaux's ribs and squeeze the trigger. Yet then the boats and everything would go back to the bank, the crew losing their jobs and homes—suffering of a different brand.

Worse, he would have blood on his hands, giving the boss what he wanted.

Gritting his teeth, he closed the box, tucked it under his arm, and hurried across the so-called field of honor.

The lawyer backed away when he saw Rory coming, a grim expression on his face. Mrs. Best held her husband's hand as she wept against the poor man's shoulder.

Rory avoided the wife's petticoats and knelt in the sand to take the gun from Best's fingers, but they were still curled tight around the trigger. His gaze flew to the man's face and discovered his eyes open, alive and watching him through tears.

"My apologies," Rory mumbled low, hoping Moreaux wouldn't overhear. He knew the Christian prayer, having heard it nearly a dozen times, but considered himself too lost to repeat the words with any effect.

Best's fingers refused to budge when he pried at them. "Hurts. Hurts. It's so cold-d-d." His bloodied teeth chattered, making talk difficult.

Mrs. Best sobbed louder and Rory's stomach twisted so tight he would've vomited if he'd eaten anything that morning. Experience had taught him better. Damn lawyer! He should know to carry the proper equipment to a duel.

"I have laudanum," Rory whispered, and opened the case, revealing the false bottom where he kept six bottles of the painkilling dosages. The man might live a day, maybe two, since he'd survived the blast, but he wouldn't have enough blood left to last longer.

Keeping his back to his employer, Rory popped the rubber stopper on the vile and brought the liquid to the dying man's lips. If Moreaux saw he carried such to his duels, he would make him regret it, as he considered medicines cowardly.

The woman thanked him, and the man's grip loosened on the pistol. When Rory had the weapon stowed and the gold latch fastened, he moved to get up, wanting to be away from the tears, the blood and the stench of innards, but the man spoke again, softly calling for his attention.

"Give me more. I want to die quickly." Red sprayed between his lips with each word. "Please! In exchange for more, I'll tell you something your boss wants to know. I—I knew Moreaux's wife, Eleanor."

"What about her?" Rory frowned, confused. Missing for the last thirteen years, Eleanor Moreaux was one of the few people he knew who'd ever beaten the man. Men who uttered the name of the gambler's unfaithful wife usually died at his hand. 'Course Best was all but in the grave already.

"Harold," the lady moaned. "No!"

Blood drizzled from the corner of his mouth. "She and her bastard daughter. I know where they went."

CPSIA information can be obtained at www.ICGtesting.com
Printed in the USA
LVOW11s1416020415

432955LV00004B/256/P